EDITH

❀ ❀ AND THE ❀ ❀

STOLEN FANS

*When someone stole Edith Arneau's valuable
fan collection, they picked the wrong victim...*

EVE PARSONS

EDITH

🐚 🐚 AND THE 🐚 🐚

STOLEN
FANS

When someone stole Edith Arneau's valuable
fan collection, they picked the wrong victim...

EVE PARSONS

MEREO
Cirencester

Mereo Books

1A The Wool Market Dyer Street Cirencester Gloucestershire GL7 2PR
An imprint of Memoirs Publishing www.mereobooks.com

Edith and the Stolen Fans: 9781861515179

First published in Great Britain in 2015
by Mereo Books, an imprint of Memoirs Publishing

The address for Memoirs Publishing Group Limited can be found at
www.memoirspublishing.com

The Memoirs Publishing Group Ltd Reg. No. 7834348

The Memoirs Publishing Group supports both The Forest Stewardship Council®
(FSC®) and the PEFC® leading international forest-certification organisations. Our
books carrying both the FSC label and the PEFC® and are printed on FSC®-certified
paper. FSC® is the only forest-certification scheme supported by the leading
environmental organisations including Greenpeace. Our paper procurement policy
can be found at www.memoirspublishing.com/environment

Typeset in 9/14pt Century Schoolbook
by Wiltshire Associates Publisher Services Ltd. Printed and bound in Great Britain
by Printondemand-Worldwide, Peterborough PE2 6XD

Chapter 1

"Edith Arneau! Did you have to climb this far?"

Mounting the steps she had fetched for the rescue, Maree grasped Edith's outstretched arms and eased her down between the lower branches of the tree. "What were you thinking of? Suppose you had fallen? Matron would be horrified."

"Matron does not have to know, Maree," Edith said as her feet touched the ground. "She has no time for me or my exercises, you should say nothing to her."

And this was why, Maree thought, as her own feet reached the grass beneath the tree. Matron was reasonably tolerant, but she would be cross if she found one of her elderly residents in this situation.

Now came the familiar downward tilt of the head, a pout to the lips and traces of the French accent, always more pronounced in her gentle voice when on the defensive. Tiny dark blue eyes sparkled under half-closed lids as she pretended meekness.

"I knew you would be returning at four o'clock," said Edith. "I did not try to get down without help. If you had not seen me I would call to you, for I wish also to speak to you privately please."

Maree refolded the steps and laid them beneath the tree. The gardener would wonder why they were there, but he'd put them away later. Despite her slight build, sixty-four year old Edith was quite capable of climbing any of the broadleaf trees gracing the gardens, though getting down often proved more difficult.

"We can talk now" Maree said. "We are alone."

Hastily glancing around, Edith shook her head. Maree was Assistant Matron at Oaklands, a large, imposing Georgian building which had been adapted to sheltered individual flats for widows. It was immaculately run by the Matron, Daphne Mitchell, and her qualified staff, and residents were well aware of Matron's, and Maree's, daily routine.

Maree's break lasted two hours, which gave ample time for lunch from an excellent Oaklands kitchen served in the staff dining room once the residents had eaten and returned to their rooms. She would then take a short walk out of Truro city into tree-lined lanes, or through the main shopping area, picking up the odd article for residents who were unable, or unwilling on the day, to do their own errands. Occasionally, as today, Maree stayed to listen to musicians playing outside the cathedral. It usually took ten minutes to get back to Oaklands. She had cut it fine today, not leaving until the last note had been played by a fine quartet.

Skirting the immaculately laid-out flowerbeds set in well-kept grassland and guiding her past the oaks after which the house had been named, Maree steered Edith to the side entrance. It was difficult to be stern with her, she mused. Most of the scrapes this feisty little lady got into were the results of her gregarious, adventure-seeking nature.

Maree gently pushed Edith ahead of her. As she entered through the side door, she noticed that Edith's expensive dark blue blazer and grey box-pleated skirt were spotted with dried lichen and tiny bits of bark. Her short softly-waved silver hair was flecked with withered leaves.

"You're in a mess Edith, and you were out of bounds again!" she scolded. "You should not be exercising out of doors."

Brushing off the debris, she asked herself how one could keep the widow of a French cartographer, after all the treks into wild mountainous countryside he must have taken her on, from continuing a hazardous lifestyle when he was no longer around to care for her.

"I come here to exercise every day when you go out," Edith pouted. "If I go near the house the nosey ones look out of the window and *voilà*! Some busybody comes to take me inside. Pouf! No more exercise!" She glanced up mischievously. "I am not a goose, Maree. I do not wish to fatten up."

Behind her, concentrating on the cleaning, Maree smiled. "You should use the exercise room and our visiting coach."

"I am not a child, I am over sixty years now." Edith turned confidentially. "How can I do my high kicks with a young man standing in front of me? And before you say it, non non, I will not wear bloomers, and trousers are for men. I have much nicer legs. I do not wish to hide them."

Maree nodded, opening her mouth to agree.

"And do not mention culottes," said Edith sternly. "They are for old schoolteachers."

"Then you should not climb trees, Edith!" Glancing at her watch, she took Edith's arm. "Come along, we must go in or I shall be late on duty."

Standing in grounds occupying a substantial corner site, the Oaklands building had three means of access. The main entrance had a drive wide enough for large cars to turn into it, enabling them to park outside the front door, giving passengers space to alight. Paths off the drive veering to right and left continued on to the car park and exited at the rear. Maree and her charge were standing on the path to the right. Here there were side doors to the house giving private access for staff or residents using the gardens.

3

As they entered Edith straightened her back, raising her voice.

"I am going to my rooms," she said with a cheeky wink, giving a fair imitation of Matron in one of her officious moments. "I shall not expect to be disturbed again today, unless by your good self. Come to call on me at five-thirty please."

Banking on Maree not reporting the tree climbing, all five feet of Edith sailed majestically through the open double doors to the residents' quarters. Maree shook her head at the retreating back. She needed to speak seriously to Edith, and soon. There was still the incident of her attempt to shin down a drainpipe because, she claimed, she was being threatened by a couple of other residents watching her each time she went out through the door. Two ladies shared the same floor, Maud Greenwood and Doreen Poirot. There'd been no trouble with them except for the odd remark regarding Edith's activities. As opposed to antagonism, they were admiring her audacity and wishing they had half her agility.

Edith continued to occupy Maree's thoughts as, having changed from her outdoor clothing into her uniform of rose-coloured smock and soft canvas shoes, she made her way to the communal lounge where the residents liked to spend time together. A large, well-furnished room, with many individual armchairs, plus side tables of varying heights, it also sported a television set and an electric organ for the musically minded. Entertainments, talks, demonstrations, all took place in the lounge, but Edith showed little interest.

Maree sighed. Why was Edith so restless? Heaven forbid that she should sit idly in her own rooms all day, but her activities, which had been looked on formerly as mild tomboy pranks, were now bothering them, and Matron still didn't know all she got up to.

Occasionally Edith had spoken of the French theatre, of having been one of its youngest stars in its heyday. Like many teenage girls of the day she'd had her heroines, enjoying nothing so much as spending her leisure hours following her favourites from theatre to theatre. Not always able to afford the entrance fee to see the show, she would gather information from discarded programmes and overheard conversations. Could they perhaps get her involved in the local players' company, Maree pondered? It shouldn't be difficult to discover where they met in Truro.

In the lounge some ladies were reading, while others were occupied with small items of handicraft or watching television. A couple of them looked up smiling at Maree as she strolled through. Of the fifteen residents, only nine were occupying the lounge today. Maree stayed to chat and assist one battling with a complicated jigsaw; then, as no one else needed her help, she continued on her round.

Chapter 2

Matron was out of the office, and on the notice board was a card:

Maree, please ask Val to take over from you this evening and join me for dinner. Something to discuss with you. Matron.

After writing, *'Yes, thank you'* Maree closed the door and went on to do her stint on the reception desk, usually quiet at this time of day. What, she wondered, did 'something to discuss' mean? She hoped Simon hadn't been leaving messages for her again. He had become a pest recently. Their engagement had ended eighteen months before. After discovering where she worked, and claiming he had business in the area, he had met and made friends with Edith. How that had come about Maree had yet to find out. When he'd first started his 'I want you back' campaign, he would often call at Oaklands, waylaying her at every opportunity. If she wasn't available he'd leave, telephoning later when other members of staff were bothered into answering it and coming to find her.

Maree enjoyed working in reception. Coloured Victorian tiles on the floor, small rugs at the base of well-padded cane chairs, cream net curtains across the large windows keeping the sun from drying the lovely green plants the gardener was so proud of, gave the room a cool, tranquil air.

A fair-haired young man rose from an easy chair, hand outstretched, and Maree smiled as they shook hands. It wasn't unusual to find visitors sitting in the reception lounge. On warm days they often chose to await the resident they were calling on, who could be resting or having a meal, surrounded by the cool green foliage of the large ferns and smaller palms.

"Maree! I knew that if I waited in here you'd appear sooner or later."

"Treve! How nice to see you again, does your aunt know you've come?"

"No, no, I'll see her later, it was you I wished to speak to at this time." He smiled, indicating for her to sit nearby. She did so, curious as he continued.

"I've been wondering how Aunt Edith has been in her general health these past few weeks?" he asked.

"I can only say that she's much as usual Treve, maybe a little subdued, as though she has something on her mind. She's also been spending more time in her own rooms, but as she told me she is doing a bit of 'spring cleaning in the summer' so that too is expected. Have you reason to be concerned about her?"

"Not concerned exactly, maybe puzzled is more the term. You see I came down on Thursday and invited her out for lunch. She turned it down, something I've never known her do before. She also claimed she had to go into Falmouth for something much more important."

Maree was also surprised. "I had no idea about that. She knows I'm always prepared to take her if she asks."

"The thing was," Treve said, "I eventually persuaded her to let me drive her to Falmouth, but when we reached the Moor she asked me to stop. When I did so she got out and asked me to meet her at the same spot in two hours' time. She wouldn't say where she was going. It's not like her to be so secretive."

"No, I agree with you, but I can only repeat, I've not noticed any great change recently. I'll keep a closer eye on her for a while and if there should be anything to concern us I'll have a word with Matron."

"Thanks, Maree. She had no shopping when she returned so it's probably nothing of any importance, but if you are able to give a little more attention for a day or two without her realising you are watching her, I'd be easier in my mind."

"I'll do my best Treve. It's good of you to care, but you are right about not letting her know, she's such an independent lady."

"That of course comes from her background. She's had to look after herself for so long she now doesn't expect anyone else to care about what interests her. Ah! here comes Matron Daphne."

As the car driven by the Oaklands porter slowly cruised toward the front entrance Maree rose, thoughtfully moving to behind the reception desk. The outer door opened and Matron entered. "Mr Hocking, how lovely!" They shook hands. "You are a few days earlier than I expected."

"I had a call that my car could be given an MOT this week," he said. "I want it done before taking my aunt to wherever she chooses to go. When they offered the use of a courtesy car I decided to take advantage of a few days owed to me to pay her a visit. Is all prepared?"

"I've not spoken to Maree yet, I intended telling her of the situation over dinner tonight." She turned to Maree. "Is it arranged with Val?"

"Val is on duty this evening anyway, Matron," Maree answered.

"Good," Matron said, turning back to Treve. "Your aunt declined to join me for dinner, but she has promised to be with us for coffee. She's been a little down this last few days but she's looking forward to her trip, that I can tell you, though she's not revealed where she wants to go."

Placing her shopping bag on the desk, she sat on Maree's vacated chair. "Has she mentioned a preference to you, Maree?"

"No. I didn't realise she was going anywhere."

"In that case, you run along and I'll see you later in the dining room." To Treve she added, "We should be eating at seven, if you could amuse yourself until then and would care to join us. Where are you staying, by the way?"

Maree heard his reply as she left reception. "The Cranwell, as usual." Not far from us then, she thought. The Cranwell, a quiet privately-run hotel, one of the larger properties close by, was conveniently situated for the use of visitors to Oaklands who wished to remain in the vicinity overnight. There were no facilities for males in Oaklands, so this neighbouring property had proved ideal.

Glancing at her watch, Maree realised she just had time to lay out her clothes for dinner before going along to Edith's rooms. While she busied herself she thought about Treve's request. Because of their recent loss and Oaklands possibly being the first time the ladies had had to look after themselves for many years, their first interview was kept short and questions were discreet. Once they'd settled in, should they require private time, Matron allowed two afternoons per week when her office was open for them. As far as she knew, Edith had never availed herself of this opportunity.

Edith welcomed her with tea and biscuits. The room was comfortable, with easy chairs strategically placed so that anyone sitting in them could speak and listen to their neighbour without difficulty, a necessity when elderly friends visited, Edith maintained. On a small table set to one side was a stack of coloured postcards.

"Has Matron spoken to you about going on a holiday?" Edith asked.

Maree muttered something about Matron not recalling all the details. She made no mention of the nephew's visit.

"Oh!" Edith nodded. "I will talk to her tonight, we will have coffee together." She reached for the postcards. "Are you interested in the theatre, Maree? I would like to show you these."

To Maree's surprise they were photographs of Victorian variety artistes in costumes of roles played. At first glance Maree was impressed with the youthful age of the stars.

"Yes I'm interested," she replied. "Where were these taken?" They were obviously posed professionally, and, by someone who knew about show business. She was delighted Edith had chosen to bring up the subject that had been on her own mind for some days.

Edith came around the table, indicating the card Maree was looking at. "That was taken in London, at the Drury Lane Theatre. I had many friends there. It's Zena Dare. She played the leading role with her sister Phyllis in *Babes in the Wood*."

She glanced at the next card Maree turned over. "Ah! The beautiful Maude Fealey, from Memphis in America. She was only three years of age when she first became a star."

"Really, so young?" Maree was impressed.

"Yes. For some of her roles over the years, and many of her long-running successes, she travelled as far away as South Africa."

Maree continued to leaf through the pack with Edith commenting until she found one of Edith herself, who modestly turned away, seemingly not wanting to answer questions about her own role on the stage. Her petite figure was dressed in a high-necked, heavily-flounced frock in burgundy, with split sleeves from shoulder to elbow. Bodice, sleeves and skirt flounces were all adorned with pink bows, and the whole was topped off with a large-brimmed burgundy bonnet trimmed with pale burgundy flowers. On her feet were a pair of burgundy boots with tiny pink buttons. The card informed its reader that, under the name of Mariette, the subject of the photo had sung in comic operas of the era in French theatres. She also created many successful roles in the Théâtre des Variétés, and was popular in Paris and all the major cities. The reverse of the card was crammed full of detail. It revealed that

Edith had, on occasions, been on loan to other theatres, including English ones.

"These postcards are lovely, Edith. Are you still interested in the theatre?"

"Oh yes. I have talked many times to the people in Truro, but although they promise to get in touch when the latest production is finished, nobody does so."

Fascinated with so much to take in, Maree had forgotten to check the time. When she did so it was twenty minutes past six.

"I must leave you now and go dress for dinner," she said.

"But I have not talked to you about what I wished to say," Edith pleaded.

"Will it keep for another day?"

"Maybe it will" Edith pouted. "Are you sure you cannot stay for just a little bit longer?" She took the postcards from Maree. "You shall look at them again next time you visit."

Maree looked at her watch. "Well, perhaps ten minutes then."

Edith sat down next to her. "Today I have to tell you about my beautiful fans who go walkabout by themselves."

"You mean you have mislaid them?"

"I do not know where they are. I search and they are not in the correct place."

"Who else knows where they are kept? Incidentally, what sort of fans are they?" Maree queried.

"They are fans to hold in the hand." Edith reached for one of the postcards. Turning her hand over, with the card held demurely under her eyes covering her nose and mouth, she made a coquettish picture. Maree was impressed. She was sure Edith's acting abilities would have been valued in some stage performances.

"I collected them for using on the stage," Edith continued. "Some time you must look at my scrapbook. You will see many pictures of my fans in use."

Maree smiled at the concerned Edith. "Next time you must tell me more. If you don't find them I will help you search for them."

Edith shook her head. "I think maybe I talk too much and somebody remembers."

"Then before I come again you must think hard who you might have talked to. Maybe we can trace them and do something about it. Now I must leave you until another time."

Chapter 3

Dressing in her room, Maree recalled her first encounter with Matron Daphne. They'd met at a training cottage hospital. Discovering they were both from the West Country, Daphne from Exmouth, herself from Dawlish, and were to take their finals in the same month, they'd agreed to keep in touch, and this had resulted in her working here now.

Fastening a silver bracelet on to her wrist, Maree glanced at the clock; two minutes to seven. Hastily she checked her make-up and hurried downstairs. Treve, having arrived early, was already sitting in the lounge, drink in hand. His taste in clothing added style to his amiable personality. Immaculately-cut beige trousers were topped off with a light brown sports jacket, over a cream shirt and brown Paisley cravat. Brown sandals covering fawn socks completed the ensemble. Like his aunt he had dark blue eyes. He smiled, showing teeth white against the enviable tan. Tall, six foot plus a couple of inches and slim, with fair wavy hair, his healthy good looks made her wonder what he did for a living.

He had not taken his eyes from her. Was it approval she read there, as he took in the royal blue calf-length dress? Her mother insisted that at five foot ten she needed clothing which was all of a piece, no odd mix and match suits. A favourite since buying it last year, the dress hugged her figure, making a welcome change from the loose smock-like garments all the Oaklands staff wore when on duty. It also set off her naturally blonde hair and fair complexion.

Matron, well built, always compact and tidy, wore a long caramel-coloured evening skirt and a cream mandarin-style blouse over which hung a gold locket. At her throat was a large gold filigree-edged brooch, at its centre an amber stone. This, Maree knew, had been a present from her husband, who had sadly died when the basket of the hot-air balloon in which he was riding had broken up in mid-air. It was with the compensation money from the accident that Oaklands had been purchased and set up.

This evening Matron seemed extra cheerful presiding over this small dinner party, and after the meal Maree learned the reason for the special occasion. Edith had requested leave of absence for a short holiday.

"She asks that you go with her, Maree," Matron said.

"Me? But why?" replied Maree, incredulous. "I'm hardly a personal friend. I look out for her, fetch a few oddments back from the shops now and then and occasionally have coffee with her in her room, but as for her wanting me to go away with her, I can't think why she should."

Matron looked at Treve. "Has she no one, Treve? Friend? Cousin? Someone she's fond of?"

Treve shook his head. "There is only me, no one else. I doubt that she would agree anyway. Once Aunt Edith has made up her mind, then that's that."

Matron accepted Treve's reply hesitantly before saying, "Living as they do in their own apartments and caring for themselves they should be capable of taking vacations alone, but technically she would still be under our care and we are responsible for her welfare. Perhaps it is too much expecting her to travel without the female company of someone she is familiar with."

"But why me?" Maree was puzzled.

"Apparently you are the only one who'll put up with her tantrums and misbehaviour."

It was doubtful Edith would have said this to Matron, though Maree often wondered how much was known of Edith's escapades in the office.

"I'm reminded too of her persistent aggravation of Mrs Poirot," said Matron.

Maree laughed. "Yes, she is naughty, she will insist on calling the poor woman Mrs Parrot or Mrs Polly. In fact with her background Edith can more easily pronounce 'Poirot' than any of our other residents."

Maree knew some of the ladies felt it was their duty to report odd goings-on, but she and Val tried to keep the peace by avoiding bothering Matron unnecessarily.

There was no time to comment further. The door behind them opened, and they all turned. Framed in the doorway was Edith, dressed in a peach floral chiffon suit that emphasised a pale, anxious face. Surely she couldn't be that concerned about discussing her forthcoming trip, Maree thought?

Rising, she made her way toward Edith, taking her arm. As she got closer she noticed Edith's eyes were glistening with unshed tears. Concerned, she asked, "What is it, Edith?"

"I was right, they've gone, all of them gone."

"What has gone?" she asked, seating Edith in an easy chair.

"My fans, all my beautiful fans! What am I to do? They are my... my personal memories. Somebody must help, please, we should look for them."

Maree glanced quickly at Treve, whose face was full of concern. It was as well they'd reached the end of the meal. Whilst she comforted Edith, Matron rang the bell, and dining room staff came to clear away the dishes followed by a waitress with coffee. Pouring a cup for Edith, Matron indicated to Treve to help himself.

The hot drink seemed to be calming Edith, but Maree refrained from asking questions, though she felt she was due some answers before deciding on a holiday with complete strangers. Now it seemed the loss of Edith's fans would complicate things even more. She must have decided when she agreed to join them that evening that she would mention them herself. But Edith would not want to be making decisions regarding a holiday after this. Edith though, had other ideas. Seemingly she'd no intention of allowing it to upset her plans.

"Did you make arrangements about the holiday?" Her voice held little trace of the anxiety that must had been racking her small frame.

"We'll talk about it in the morning," Matron said quietly.

"But I shall sleep with more peace if we talk about it now."

"I will go with you." Playfully Maree punched her arm. "You need someone to keep you under control. Where shall we go? St Ives? Weston-Super-Mare?"

"I want to go to France."

"France!" Maree echoed. "But I know nothing of France."

"Then I must teach you, you will adore it." She smiled. "And all those handsome French men, ooh la la, they will love you. We will have a good time, you and me."

"But I... I..." She looked up. Treve was watching them. What was on his mind? Did he think she was being over-familiar with his aunt? She recalled her earlier thoughts. It would still be necessary to speak seriously to Edith. Perhaps this trip would give her an opportunity. If she was determined to go to France, hopefully Treve would drive them at least part of the way, and if she timed it right, she'd speak while he was still with them. When he knew why she needed to persuade Edith to take more responsibility for her actions, he might even add his own arguments. She was sure he'd have something to say regarding his aunt's escapades.

"How far into France would we go?" she asked.

"I wish to call at the removal firm who bring me to England." Edith nodded. "Maybe my cabinet of fans will still be in the hold of the ferryboat and they will look for them."

"Do you remember who they were?" Treve voiced his concern "It was eighteen months ago, they may not still be in business."

"Of course I remember," Edith was quick to reply. "They are a reliable company with good business in Montpellier, they would not close and lose it. I will telephone tomorrow. I will ask."

"But you must understand," Treve persisted. "The firm would have its own furniture wagons which would have been loaded at the depot in France and travelled on the ferry as they were. Nothing would have been taken off and put into the hold."

"How can you be so sure, Treve? You were not there on the day I left my beautiful France to travel to this country."

"That is true aunt, but it is not normally how the ferry works. Besides, did you not leave from Lyon?"

"You are right." Edith nodded. But the wagon came from Montpellier. I tell you I will ring tomorrow."

"Edith and Luc lived in a village near Lyon," Treve said, joining them. "Both of us are familiar with Montpellier. Unfortunately it is a long drive through France." He shrugged, looking at Maree. "Some of the roads are in beautiful countryside, some fairly rugged it's true, hilly, mountainous even, hence Luc's attraction for the area as his home. On the other hand there are good snack-eating places and well-run restaurants, so you won't starve. People travel from all over the country, but unless you know the area, driving can be difficult."

"I would wish to visit Strasbourg," said Edith. "There is a good costume and gift shop, I remember."

Maree shook her head, her concern evident. "Isn't that where

The European Parliament is held? And I believe the Council of Europe."

"Yes," Treve agreed, "but you can keep away from the busiest parts, there is a large area for pedestrians only, including a mini train service."

As she sipped her own coffee, Maree was concerned. Driving in strange territory for the first time, she couldn't possibly undertake to get them there and back with no problems. She thought of visiting somewhere nearer home, but realised she couldn't say so. As a guest, she would be expected to go where her hostess went - and there were Edith's fans to think of now.

"What about it, Treve? How do you see it?" Matron asked.

He nodded. "I had intended accompanying them as far as the ferry if my aunt chose to travel abroad, but after what Maree has said I know my conscience would bother me if I let it rest there. How would you feel, Maree, if I tagged along as chauffeur?"

Maree thought before replying. This could be ideal. Perhaps Treve would then be in a position to witness first-hand his aunt's erratic behaviour. She smiled.

"More than happy, Treve, but are you sure we would not be taking you away from something important?"

"That depends on when we are to set off." He placed his arm affectionately across his aunt's shoulders. "It's been some time since Aunt Edith suggested we had a few days away and of course you won't know, Maree, I'm the curator of our local museum. In a few weeks it will be closed for three months while we lend some of our exhibits to another museum which will be celebrating an anniversary year."

"I see, so then would be a good time for you to be away?"

"Yes," Treve nodded. "But I'd like to know more about those missing fans, it might be worth including enquiries for them in our itinerary."

Matron rose, interrupting. "I'm taking Edith to the office.

There are procedures to be followed when something goes missing at Oaklands. Come along, Edith. You can talk about your arrangements later."

A subdued Edith trailed quietly behind Matron. As the door closed Treve suggested another coffee. He stood to pour, not waiting for a reply.

"Of all the things Aunt Edith could be accused of, being careless with her possessions isn't one of them," he said. "She has always been most vigilant."

"It puzzles me too," Maree said. "But perhaps if you had seen her as Matron did on the morning of her arrival here, you might think otherwise."

"Oh?"

"Yes." Maree smiled. "Apparently your aunt was expected to arrive on the London train about noon. Instead, when the doors were unlocked in the morning she was discovered outside the front entrance sitting on her suitcases surrounded by overflowing Harrods bags, nonchalantly eating an apple."

Treve laughed, nodding. "I can see her doing that. She'd not have dreamt of disturbing the house too early."

"She'd been there for an hour, she told them. Had any joggers come out for a morning run she would have joined them, she said. This was at seven o'clock. I assume she would have left her luggage where it stood!"

"So, did she travel by overnight train, to arrive so early?"

Thoughtfully Maree reached for her cup. It was obvious Edith had not confided in her nephew at the time.

"Your aunt travelled down from Bristol in the cab of a furniture wagon" she told him, sipping her coffee.

"Why doesn't that surprise me?" Treve replaced his own cup on the table. "Though I do wonder what she was thinking of, being at a loose end and alone in a strange city in the early hours of the morning." He shook his head, puzzled.

"Apparently she had arrived there by coach and on discovering she had a two-hour stopover before the next stage she'd taken a chance and asked the wagon driver where he was going. On learning that it was Truro she asked him to take her on."

"I wonder what he thought of that?" Treve smiled. "I can't imagine he'd get many requests from elderly ladies begging lifts."

"Edith thought it was great," Maree assured him as she stood up to place her used coffee cup and saucer on to the tray. "She'd had the time of her life, she said, and never enjoyed a journey so much."

"And did this driver wait with her until they took her in? Or did he clear off, together with a bag or two?"

Treve had reason to be suspicious, she told herself as she sat down again; he must have thought his aunt had been conned out of her treasure before today and nobody cared enough to do anything about it.

Maree answered him honestly. "Yes, he'd gone by the time they'd got her and her luggage inside, but she insisted he was a very nice man. She claims he helped her out of the cab and then passed out all her luggage. Apparently he also gave her his address and phone number in case she wanted to go back by the same route. That doesn't sound like a man who was planning to rob her, does it?"

Before he could answer, Matron returned. "Edith has gone to her room," she said as she sat down. "She asks if you would call in before going to your own bed, Maree." She turned to Treve. "I offered her something to help her sleep, but she refused. Your aunt is one tough lady, Treve. Not many of her age would accept the loss of personal, precious items without having hysterics."

Treve nodded. "She never has been one to panic. Her resilience has helped her overcome many setbacks through the years." He nodded towards Maree. "We've been discussing the best way to find out what has actually happened. Perhaps tomorrow she will remember something that helps."

Matron nodded. "I'm relieved you've agreed to chauffeur them if the trip still goes ahead. I shall feel much easier in my mind with you at the wheel."

Treve picked up the coffee pot, indicating to Matron that there was more coffee if she wanted it. She shook her head, smiling her thanks. Replacing the pot, Treve continued.

"You know her as the demure little gentlewoman, but at fifteen her boyish escapades caused her parents real heartache, and they were unable to control her. It was thought a spell of proper discipline would do the trick."

"And did it, Treve?"

"I can't say, Daphne. Who knows what would have happened if the promise that she could return from France to England when she reached her sixteenth birthday had been kept?

"In those days a natural follow-up would probably have been for her to go into service," Matron said thoughtfully before rising. "Perhaps that's what her parents had in mind. But to some extent that clarifies certain things for me. Now I am going to leave you. When you've finished with the coffee perhaps you'd ring for the staff to collect the trays, etcetera. I'll say goodnight, Treve. I will see you in the morning, Maree."

Treve rose, and with a "Goodnight Matron", placed the remaining dishes on to the tray, before crossing to ring the bell.

"What about a stroll, Maree?

"Yes, thank you Treve, that would be lovely."

Chapter 4

The evening air was warm, and no coats were necessary as they left by the side door joining the path leading to the front entrance.

"So what did Edith do when she realised she wouldn't be able to come home?" Maree asked. "Was she able to stay on at the school?"

"No, without the proper fees being paid there was no way they could keep her on. Aunt Edith was forced into finding work."

"Presumably she would also have had to find somewhere to live?" Maree said, matching her steps to his. "What on earth did she do?"

"She chose the stage. At that time the variety theatres were constantly on the lookout for talented youngsters. They were also prepared to house and train them in the art of all things to do with the subject."

Treve stopped as they reached one of the seats overlooking the garden. He didn't sit, but stood behind it.

"Of course she would have been with others of her own age," Maree said. "She must have been much happier."

"True," Treve agreed, "and to give her her due, even with all the mischief, she had always been good at the performing arts at school."

"What about her parents? Did they approve or help in any way?" Maree didn't think there would have been help, but hoped that once Edith had showed she could stand on her own two feet there might have been a family reconciliation.

"No," Treve told her. "They didn't consider the theatre a fit place for females, either for working or visiting. It had the effect of alienating her even more."

That accounted for many things not readily understood about her, Maree thought. Aloud she said. "So, no real family life or anyone to care for her after the age of fifteen?"

"No, though according to my mother, she became well loved for herself as well as an actress. Her presence was always being requested at functions large and small, and her singing regularly had the audiences begging encores."

Turning away from the seat, he squeezed her arm. "Shall we walk?" He indicated the front gates, which were fastened back. Through the gates they turned to the right, away from the city and along the tree-lined avenue.

"I enjoy walking under the trees at this time of year," Maree said. "The gentle rustling makes them sound as though they are pleased to be full of leaf again after the long winter."

"So you too are an old romantic?" He took her hand.

"Not so much of the old, if you please!" She laughed, liking the comfort of her hand in his. "Carry on with your aunt's story. How long was she employed in the theatre?"

"Ten to twelve years. When she was eighteen she met and married Luc Arneau. He was an up and coming cartographer, well respected. His work was considered good by those who used it."

"Did the family attend the wedding?" Maree asked.

"She wrote to the family beforehand, inviting them to attend a civil ceremony. They declined, but they did sign the necessary permits. My mother maintained they saw their opportunity of getting rid of the responsibility. Luc's family too cried off, as they resented his refusal to take any active part in the family business."

"Oh dear, what sort of business was it?"

"Wine making. They ran a vineyard as well as owning a château that was let to another branch of the family who ran it as a hotel. I understand that Luc had been primed from an early age to take over that side of the business, so when he defected, to travel and explore the mountains, his family were more than disappointed."

"Obviously," Maree said quietly. "But it didn't put them off marrying?"

"No, but with no family support they needed to save money, so to still achieve their heart's desire, the pair went off with only a couple of friends as witnesses."

How sad. Maree hoped that if ever she married her whole family would be in attendance, even if it was only the simplest of ceremonies. She wondered - had Edith been in England, would she have run away to Gretna Green in Scotland, marrying over the blacksmith's anvil? How romantic that would have been for them.

"Did her family stay in touch? Perhaps I should ask if Edith stayed in touch with them."

"She wrote once or twice, mainly requesting financial help. I'm afraid she didn't get it. Rather, it made them disown her altogether."

"Are they both gone now?"

They had reached a gate leading to a park. Stopping, he released her hand, resting both of his on the top bar before replying.

"Both parents died when she was in her forties, her mother first. Her father lived another three years. He had relented somewhat in that he left her a legacy in the care of my mother. It was only to be paid if Edith was in real need, otherwise it was to go to charity. The decision was entirely my mother's as she was Edith's only cousin. She did send them money included in the legacy that had come to her, but said nothing of that left specifically for Edith. "

"How generous" Maree said. "Your mother sounds a very nice lady."

"Like yourself, my mother has a caring personality. She had never agreed to the treatment meted out to Edith, insisting her behaviour was no more than adolescent high spirits - look!" He broke off, pointing across the park, "See, over there, under that tree in the corner, creeping along under the hedge. See it?" He pulled her to him. "A fox! They are so daring now, no fear of humans any more, have they?"

"We do see one taking a short cut through Oaklands garden and the car park occasionally," she told him, happy to share his moment of boyish excitement.

He pulled up a sleeve, glancing at his watch. "Time to go, if we don't want to wake the residents when we return." He placed an arm around her shoulders, drawing her close. "I've enjoyed this evening." He turned her to face him. "I would very much like to see you again. Could we perhaps have dinner on our own some time?"

"I'm sure that could be arranged. We're going to meet soon anyway to discuss the trip."

They settled to a comfortable stroll, his arm remaining across her shoulders.

"What happened to Edith's husband?" she queried tentatively. "Was it his heart?" She had never liked to ask Edith.

"No, he had a serious fall down a mountainside. One of the Jura group in France. He was badly injured and spent months in the hospital. Edith finally insisted she cared for him at home with the help of a qualified nurse."

"Did his family help?" Maree asked, though she guessed what the answer would be.

"No," he said. "It only made them resent her more. In fact they suggested that if he hadn't taken the step of marrying a foreigner he would not have had the accident."

She stopped, turning to him. "How awful, and Edith with no one of her own to talk to." She glanced up at him. "What about the property, has it been sold? Or is it still there for her to return to?"

"All but a few personal items, which are Edith's property anyway, have of course been passed to the family."

"Does that mean..." She stopped mid-sentence, reluctant to delve any further into something that was none of her business. Treve, realising her dilemma. filled in for her.

"Because of the French inheritance laws the female, or widow, inherits only the right to live in the family home. The children are the real inheritors." He paused. "You are not familiar with the French customs?"

Maree shook her head. "No, and I didn't mean to pry."

"It's as well you know a little of the country you will be visiting," he said. "So, to continue, the children inherit in equal shares, and as this extends to the children of the first children and so on down the line, and all of them have to be in complete agreement before the property can be sold, you can imagine the difficulties involved."

Maree shook her head, "Complicated, to say the least. But what about the property that belongs to Edith?" She felt a strong bond of sympathy with his aunt at the thought of someone holding on to what, after all, were Edith's personal items, nothing to do with vineyards or châteaux.

"Supposing it were to be sold?" she asked anxiously. "How would she know? Do the people in France know where to find her?"

Treve stopped, turning her to him. "My aunt is very lucky to be looked after by you." He smiled down at her. "But to answer your query, Luc's family won't need to be involved. A solicitor has the information necessary, and all her property is safely stored in premises owned by him. He has sole vending rights and nothing could be sold without going officially through him."

They had almost reached the gates. Maree said, "It's nice to know someone is there for Edith." Looking up at the house, she added, "I hope she is sleeping peacefully now."

As they turned in at the gate, Treve laughed quietly. "Not much chance of that, I'm afraid. Look!"

Edith was standing in the main doorway, a light brown jacket over the suit she'd worn earlier. So she had not gone to bed after all.

"Edith, were you waiting for us?" Maree said as they reached her. "I hope we haven't kept you from your bed?"

"No, I am not sleepy, though Matron expects me to be. I think I will take some of the evening air. I did not know you young people would be out here in the garden. I think I will be alone." She linked arms with them, turning them once again to face the front gate. "We will sit on a seat together and talk to each other."

"If that is what you wish, Aunt," Treve said, guiding them to the path on the left. "We'll not want to be too near the front of the house. Will this do?" They were approaching a seat partly surrounded by hydrangea shrubs.

"Yes, it is good," Edith said, as they settled themselves. "We will be cosy and quiet, to talk with comfort."

"Have you something particular you want to talk about, Aunt?" Treve glanced at his watch. "it is almost ten o'clock, I do not want to keep you ladies from your beauty sleep."

"But it is I who keep us here, Treve." Edith tapped her nephew's arm. "I think maybe Maree is not so happy about coming to France with us because she does not know where she will be taken." She turned to Maree, taking her friend's hand in her own. "Have no fears, Maree, we will not leave you alone and Treve will be an excellent escort for us both when we visit the beautiful towns and cities."

"Oh, but I did not mean to imply - I thought that maybe you would want to visit a relative, or - or - that someone might wish to visit you…" Maree found it difficult to put her meaning into words. After what she had learned of Edith's unhappy times in France, she did not feel she could easily meet or be comfortable with any of the relatives who had been the cause of her unhappiness.

"Sadly there are no relatives close to me in France, Maree, I have only business to be settled in that country now and I must wait for someone to get in touch with me about it. Is that not so, Treve?"

"Have you heard nothing concerning the sales yet?" Treve asked. "perhaps we could look into it when we are over there. After all it will be summer and if those items are to be sold, now is the time."

"We cannot spend so much time on the business, Treve" said Edith. "We are to go on a holiday."

"It will take only minutes to enquire at the solicitors if they have the boat on show in the harbour," her nephew said. "The wheelchair and specially-adapted scooter are bound to take longer, but no doubt they will continue to be entered in local auction sales. I will look into it myself while you ladies are shopping one day, perhaps."

"You have a boat?" Maree asked Edith. "Did you and your husband sail?"

"No, sadly it is a boat which has been only a few times to the water, Maree." Edith turned to Treve. "You will tell Maree the circumstances."

"Are you sure you want to be reminded of those difficult times, Aunt?"

Edith tapped him on the knee. "Maree is my friend, and those times are my past life which she does not know."

"Very well, then I will make it as brief as I can. Come and sit next to me, Maree."

Maree chose to sit between Treve and his aunt. Surreptitiously he tucked her arm in his. "When Aunt Edith's father died he left her a substantial sum of money in the custody of her sister, my mother, to be paid only if she was in dire straits. That need arose when Luc, her husband, had a serious accident on a mountain..."

"He was never to walk again," Edith interrupted.

"And so, of course, unable to work either," Treve said.

"How sad for you both." Maree gently squeezed Edith's hand. "How did you manage?"

"Oh, but I did have help," Edith replied. "I have the hospital nurse who comes to bath and dress my poor sick Luc. I am able to shop when she is there and cook and clean the house when she has gone for the first time. At night she returns to care for him again and to prepare him for the bed. I was very lucky. I also have the needlework. It kept me busy when all household chores are done." She sighed. "Ooh, such lovely costumes I worked on for my friends the theatre ladies."

"That," Treve said, "was when mother decided to give Edith the legacy left by her father. She hoped it might make life a little easier for them."

"I did not agree to take his money at first." Edith shook her head. "I thought he would not help when he was alive, so why should I use his money after he was no longer with us?"

"True" Treve said. "My aunt was a little angry at first, refusing to take it, but in the end she decided to use it to try making Luc's life easier. By employing a daily help, it gave her more time to spend with him. Hiring a chauffeur-driven car for trips to the coast, sometimes taking a friend with them as male company for Luc, and wasn't that when you bought the boat, Aunt?"

"My husband taught me to sail and navigate in the French waters when we were so much younger," Edith offered. "We had many happy days when he did not climb mountains." She paused thoughtfully. "Now that he could do so little for himself I expected that it would give him a wider horizon to think about in his quiet moments."

"No doubt he enjoyed it too." Maree took Edith's hand in her own, holding on to it this time.

"Unfortunately, he never did get strong enough to take the roll of the waves without someone, or an especially fitted harness, to hold him in position," Treve said.

"He made many strong objections to any assistance," Edith added, sighing softly. "Ah, my poor Luc. He did not like being so helpless."

What a difficult time Edith would have had if Luc had survived, Maree thought. Perhaps she'd have returned to England sooner, bringing him with her.

"I'm sure he could not have been cared for in better hands, Edith. Sadly you were not able to keep him for long."

"We shared twenty-five years of happiness and love" Edith said quietly as she rose from the seat. "I have no regrets, and I know Luc had none. He always assured me how happy he was." She turned to, Maree. "Only when the pain was severe was he unhappy." She shook her head. "Then it was on my behalf, he was sorry for the extra work he was giving me."

Swallowing, Edith turned away from them, saying quietly, "I am ready for my bed. Today has been only half a good day for me. Goodnight. We will talk of the holiday another day."

Whispering "Goodnight", they watched her go. It had been a painful and emotional reminiscence for her, and they had no wish to prolong it.

Treve sighed as he placed an arm round Maree's shoulders, making sure his aunt was safely inside the door before saying, "I'd hoped that by this time all would have been settled for her. She is happy here at Oaklands. She loves having her own rooms and knowing someone is there for her is a big help. It's a pity the fans have gone missing just now." He shook his head. "We can do nothing tonight, we'll discuss it again next time we meet. He turned Maree to him. "Which I trust will be soon?"

Maree suddenly found herself embarrassed at his nearness. How did he expect her to respond? Tentatively she raised her head. He was gazing down at her intently.

"In a few days, probably," she said quietly.

"Good" he replied. "Now let's get you inside too."

Chapter 5

"Edith! Sit here." Maree indicated the space beside her on the garden bench. Edith, ignoring the suggestion, squeezed herself between Maree and Treve, smiling cheekily as surprised, they moved apart to accommodate her.

"It's been three days since we were last together, Edith," Maree said. "We are discussing the trip. Are you sure you want to go all the way to France with only me for company?"

"I want very much to go with you two nice people, my understanding friend and my favourite nephew." She squeezed Maree's hand. "What more could I ask?"

"So you know that Treve is going to drive us?"

"Yes, I always knew he would. He could not help but respond to a damsel in distress, could he?" She giggled. "I am a damsel, and do you not agree I am in distress?"

"When are we to start on this hunt-cum-holiday?" Treve inquired, ignoring his aunt's levity. "I'd hope not to be travelling through French holiday resorts during the busy season."

"Oh, but we would also make a holiday of it." A slight narrowing of the eyes as she smiled at them made Maree suspect

Edith of plotting something to suit herself.

"And maybe I meet a friend, we can have fun together."

Treve shrugged, "So you would take us to France and abandon us while you go off with your old cronies?" He pretended to be stern.

"But you will have each other to keep you occupied, you will not have time for a lady who spends precious hours looking for lost fans."

Treve rose to stand in front of Edith and took her hands. "My dear, dear aunt, if you want a day off with your friends of course you can have it. I'm sure Maree and I can amuse ourselves."

Yes, Maree agreed silently, though what that amusement might consist of she wasn't sure. Treve had earlier mentioned his ability to converse in French, much needed for the visitors to the museum, she imagined. To give him his due he was still taking lessons, but she had no language other than her own. She guessed they would have to point at what they wanted to buy, or talk only to each other.

Maree wondered about fixing a date, though it was necessary to speak to Matron and consider her holiday before her own. Perhaps she should also talk with Treve to forestall his aunt arranging it without consultation. If Edith really did have friends to meet up with, maybe they should enquire beforehand what they might like to do.

Looking at them both, she stood up. "Are you happy to let it rest there, Edith? It will be a long journey, with no guarantee you'll get your fans back."

Edith nodded. "You two have made me happy. Now I know we shall be looking for them, the fans will be less of the trouble."

She too stood, turning to Maree, kissing her on both cheeks. Then, after subjecting Treve to the same treatment, she performed a pirouette, tugging him around with her. He was obviously used to her exuberance, for he lifted her and set her aside, giving her a squeeze to demonstrate what a favourite she was to him.

"Are you sure you haven't already made arrangements to meet someone?" Maree asked. Twinkling eyes and lightness of movement gave Edith a roguish air. Keeping them guessing, Edith chose not to answer.

"Shall we meet in a few days to finalise the date of departure?" Treve asked. "I'm to pick my car up next week, so before I go home I'll drop in to see how you're doing with your arrangements. Meanwhile I will work on the route."

"Maree and I will have many clothes to pack. You will have to tell us if we are to walk on bad roads, and we will know what shoes to wear. We must also have the evening wear. The hotels will have entertainment for us to dance to. We will also take the beach clothes."

She turned to the bewildered Maree and laughed. "You will adore my France, so much to see. You think Cornwall is pretty, but wait until you see what I have to show you. You will love it. You will not want to return."

She saw Treve hovering, and addressed him quickly.

"Yes yes, Treve, we will have the talk about arrangements. When you come to see us the next time we will have it all settled. Only you will not be prepared." She punched him lightly in the midriff, laughing mischievously.

Treve gave her a gentle shake. "You are naughty, and if you don't behave Maree and I will leave you at home and go off on our own. We will forget all about you."

"Ooh, you cannot do it, there has to be a chaperone!" Edith did not look at Maree as she continued. "It would not be correct. Matron would be disagreeable."

Treve had not taken her seriously. He glanced at Maree. "Do you think you need a chaperone, Maree? Have I behaved so badly at the times we've spent together?"

There was some jocularity in his voice, but when she looked up with face burning he was poised as if wanting an answer.

"Of course I don't Treve, I'm sure I shall enjoy our trip no matter what."

Treve turned to his aunt. "There, you are, we could go without you. Maree is not in need of a chaperone."

Maree half expected Edith to respond with a laugh. Instead there was an enigmatic look on her face; she wasn't sure about Treve's threat.

"Tomorrow I will see about my clothes, and you must do the same. Then we should go into the town to purchase something new to take with us."

Maree took Edith to Truro the next afternoon in her car. She had a few misgivings when Edith chose the most expensive shops to call in and was a little diffident about her own selections, for in the end Edith chose for her: two evening dresses, one turquoise, one in delicate powder blue and white, several summer skirts in bright floral colours with plain tops to match, and finally, sports trousers and jacket, although Maree seldom wore either. Edith's argument that these would be required for sight-seeing cut very little ice with Maree. When she suggested France was warm so they wouldn't be necessary, Edith's answer was to gather them up and march to the cash desk, leaving her to pick up the already too-full shopping bag and trail of dropped goods.

Though Maree agreed with Edith's choice, she dreaded having the payment deducted from her credit card. She rushed to the counter, card in hand, but too late; Edith had an account with this lovely shop and as if the cashier was afraid they would change their minds regarding the amount they'd bought, she hastily entered it on the till roll and gave Edith the chit to sign.

"Hush," Edith said, when Maree protested. "You are doing this for me. It is right I buy you something. Shoes must be next, after we will go for the coffee and cakes. When we come out we will buy bags, shoulder bags for you, you are so tall you would not look chic with little handbag." Maree's small car had never been so laden with shopping as on her return to Oaklands that day.

It was the following Friday afternoon when Edith disappeared. Val, Maree's assistant, called to replace Edith's linen and got no reply to her knocking. Using her master key she let herself in, and not too concerned, she left the clean linen and carried on with her normal duties. It wasn't until six o'clock it was discovered that Edith had not returned to collect her key from reception. Val mentioned it to Maree when they met in the office.

"Do you realise Edith has not collected her key as yet?" she said.

Maree glanced at her watch. "She didn't mention she was going to be out this afternoon. Perhaps she's met someone in town."

It was a little after seven o'clock when Edith finally showed up, offering no explanation as to why she was later than usual.

The following Thursday Treve arrived soon after lunch. He drove them into Truro, discussing on the way final arrangements and what last-minute items they would need. That done, he dropped Edith off at the hairdresser's. After promising to pick her up in an hour or so, he and Maree went for afternoon tea. This gave her the opportunity to tell him of Edith's disappearance the previous Friday.

"I wonder if she is meeting someone we're not aware she knows," Treve suggested. "After all she could have friends in the city, maybe someone connected with the Drama group."

"Of course, that must be it," Maree said. "I'm surprised I didn't think of that myself."

The café was on the top floor of what had once served as the City Guildhall. The room's ambience with the slightly overcast light coming in through the windows added to Maree's pleasure at learning of Treve's early life in Dorset, when, in between studying, he had been employed to help look after his parent's considerable estate of forestry and farmland.

"When I was seventeen…" He broke off as the waitress arrived to take their order. "Cream teas for two please," he said with a glance at Maree, who nodded in agreement. With a "thank you sir," the waitress left them. He continued, "I uncovered a Roman relic buried in one of the fields. It was an exciting find, a dirty but rather lovely piece of jewellery, and Father sent me to the museum with it. The chief curator was extremely interested. He congratulated me on not doing anything about the dirt but leaving it to the experts to clean."

The waitress returned with a loaded tray. Treve waited until she'd served them before continuing.

"A failing with lots of finders apparently is that they cannot resist scraping and scratching. The Curator despatched it to the British Museum for assessment. I was so eager for the results to come back I plagued the life out of the staff until they'd got an answer."

"And?" Maree reached for the teapot, raising her eyebrows in question.

"Yes, it was valuable," he said. "Believed to be from the old Blandford Forum area."

"I've come across that name somewhere," she commented thoughtfully. "Did you ever learn the origin of it?"

"Yes, of course I looked it up. Bland comes from blaege, old English for gudgeon. The gudgeon is a little fish. A ford is a place where gudgeon could be caught. Forum is Latin for market place. So the relic could possibly have been a piece of jewellery lost by someone who frequented the marketplace."

She handed him his tea. "And that whetted your appetite, did it?"

"Yes, every spare minute was either spent in the museum or," he smiled as he prepared a scone with jam and cream, "as my father often remarked, I'd got my head stuck in an archaeological book. It was extremely interesting."

"I can imagine," Maree said as she too picked up a scone.

"So much so that when I finished at college, father suggested I try for a part-time job helping out at the museum on my days off from the land. I became so interested I was offered a full-time post and training in all aspects of the work." He took a bite of his scone, nodding with satisfaction. "These are good."

Maree swallowed a mouthful of her own scone. "Delicious. Home made I'd suggest." Treve nodded.

They enjoyed their food in silence until Maree had finished eating.

"So" she asked, "how did you manage to get away from your parent's property? It couldn't have been easy for them to let you go, or do you have more family involved?"

He sipped at his tea before replying. "No, I'm an only child, but to answer your question, they were selling off some of the forestry preparatory to retirement. A while later they offered to release me." Replacing his cup in the saucer he picked up the last of his scone and finishing it, put the plate to one side. "I was happy to accept the post. I still spend a great deal of time on home land with a metal detector."

Hence the tan, she thought.

He'd had several more valuable finds, he told her, but nothing to compare with the jewellery. The local history society had invited him to talk to them regarding the finds and this often resulted in his taking groups of like-minded people out on field hunts on his father's land. He was looking forward to the French trip.

"Aunt Edith is also keen on the subject, so don't be surprised if she sidles off one day once we get into the rougher, more natural countryside in France," he said. He glanced at his watch. "We'd better not be late or she'll think we really have gone off and left her behind."

Edith was waiting for them, but judging by the flushed face she had only recently come out from under the hairdryer.

Shopping completed, they arrived back at Oaklands to find Maree had a visitor waiting in reception: her sister, Barbara.

"I telephoned here, Maree," she said. "I was told you had gone shopping and wouldn't be away long."

"But what made you come all this way on impulse?" Maree asked.

"The idea came to me when Dad suggested I take the day off. There is a synod on locally and he is confined to the house with visiting clergymen for the day, so he suggested I use his car. I had no difficulty getting to Truro, but I ended up travelling several times around the city before somebody gave me the correct directions to Oaklands."

"It's wonderful to see you." They embraced and Marie made the introductions to Treve and Edith, asking, "Have you introduced yourself to Matron and Val?"

"Of course, and by the way," Barbara whispered, "you have done well for yourself, the parents will be pleased. They imagined you in some little village in the back of beyond. Just wait until I tell them."

Matron interrupted. "Excuse me, but you will stay for a meal won't you?"

"Oh, may I? I'm quite hungry!" Barbara was always hungry. Teenage hormones, her mother put it down to.

"The residents are all in their own dining room tonight," Matron told them. "I'm going out, that is unless you'd like to go out Maree?" Maree shook her head, thinking about all the time she'd be taking off soon for Edith's trip.

"Then you will have the staff dining room to yourselves. Incidentally, the whole house knows you have your sister visiting, so don't be surprised if extra staff come in with the meal, as well as one or two of the residents. They are all anxious to get a glimpse of the other Devon beauty Mark has told them about."

"Who is Mark?" Barbara whispered to Maree.

"The gardener cum porter cum handyman," she said. "A nice man, but a bit old for you."

"Oh, don't you have any young people here?"

Maree didn't reply. She hoped Barbara would go to university when her gap year was up.

Matron, as she left reception said, "I will leave you now. Have a pleasant evening." She glanced at Edith, who was fussing with her shopping bags, then raised her eyebrows at Maree, who nodded to let her know everything was well.

"Have a safe journey home, Barbara, please feel free to come again some time."

Barbara murmured her thanks as Matron left. "Gosh, she's nice isn't she?"

"I will take these to my room before the dinner is announced," Edith said, gathering her bags.

Maree picked up her own shopping. "You coming, Barbara?"

"You bet," she replied. "I want a peek into those interesting-looking bags if I have time."

Maree looked around for Treve, who had settled in an easy chair. "Back soon" she called to him.

Arriving in her sister's fairly spacious quarters, Barbara couldn't wait to turn all the packages out on to the bed. Her oohs and ahs of approval reached Maree in the bathroom, where she was lightly retouching her make-up.

"Never mind those," Maree said, arriving back at the side of the bed, "How is everything at home? Are Mum and Dad well? What about the typing? Are you still managing to cope with it all?"

"Easy peasy," Barbara said. "Dad's quite a pet to work for, though he's spoiling me for anyone else."

"Your time off is nearly up. How long are you intending this year out to be?"

"I've been offered a place at Leeds University. If I want it, I have to take it up in September."

"Oh, how lovely. You will take it won't you?"

"I think so, but there's a bit of a complication." She turned away, fussing with one of the packets on the bed.

"Oh?"

"Simon."

"Simon? Not Simon Markham?" Maree wasn't sure she'd heard correctly. "You don't mean... oh no, you can't!"

"What do you mean, I can't? You finished with him ages ago." Barbara remained leaning against the bed, her back to her sister. "He said you were playing Miss Hoity Toity and talked only of getting away from home and all its ties. Actually, he wanted to come with me today, but I wasn't sure how you'd feel about it."

"I would not have been pleased at you bringing him without giving me notice. This is my place of work, he already makes a nuisance of himself here often enough, and if I have to socialise with him again I'd rather it were away from Oaklands."

"So it's all right for me to see him then?"

"He's thirty-two, a bit old for you isn't he?"

"Only eleven years older, and anyway he's far more thoughtful than some men of my age."

Maree turned away. "We'd better go down. I'm sure the meal must be ready."

As they reached the bedroom door Maree prevented Barbara from opening it, taking her hand and turning her around.

"Be careful, Barbara, please, he has been around a good many years longer than you," she said. "I wouldn't want you to be hurt."

"Oh, I'm sure he wouldn't do anything to hurt me, and anyway what did you mean by making a nuisance of himself here? He's never said he comes to see you."

"He does call in occasionally."

Barbara looked puzzled. It was obvious Simon had not told her of his continual visits to Oaklands.

"But he claims not to know where you are."

41

This didn't surprise Maree, but she wondered how long he expected to keep it a secret when he must know that as sisters they were regularly in touch with each other.

"I'm sorry, Barbara, perhaps he didn't want to upset you."

Over dinner the talk was exciting and flowed freely. Barbara, thoughtful at first, became quite animated when the trip to France was mentioned. "When are you going? How long will you stay?" she asked. "Could I come? It would finish my year off brilliantly, just think of being able to tell my uni mates I'd been to Paris during my year out."

"What about..." Maree didn't get to finish.

"Simon? Oh I'm sure he..."

It was obvious Barbara had only one person on her mind.

"It was dad I was thinking of," Maree said. "How would he cope while you were away for maybe two weeks? Besides, don't you have to help get a new secretary installed before you go away? Do you think you could find a replacement quickly?"

"You do know how to dampen a girl's spirit, sis." Barbara was petulant during the second course, but cheered up again when Treve showed an interest in the studies she'd be doing at university. The rest of the meal passed pleasantly.

Suddenly it was nine o'clock, and Barbara stood up.

"Time to be on my way" she said. "It will take me a couple of hours to get home and I wouldn't want to cause the parents worry."

Maree rose to see her off. Treve also got up, offering a piece of paper to Barbara. "This might help you," he said.

Barbara looked at what he'd given her. "Ooh, a map of the route home. Oh, thank you. If I'd only had this on the way down I'd never have got lost."

"You'll know for next time won't you?" Treve shook hands with her. She immediately reached up on her toes to kiss his cheek. "Thank you again," she said.

Edith smiled at her, then kissed her on both cheeks. "Maybe if you are very good while we are away we will bring you home something pleasant. Then next time we have a holiday you can join us. We will go somewhere for you to enjoy."

"She's an odd biddy isn't she?" Barbara said as the sisters made their way to the car park. "She talked to me as if I was a little girl."

"Edith is a shrewd character. Maybe she thought you were too young to be out so late driving on your own. You must remember it wasn't the done thing when she was your age."

They reached the car and Barbara fished in her bag for her keys. She gave a little squeal. "Oh, oh dear!" She handed over an envelope. "I'm sorry, Maree, a letter from mum. I should have given it to you as soon as I arrived. I haven't time for you to answer it now."

Slipping the letter into her pocket, Maree said, "Tell mum I'll phone tomorrow evening."

"Oh, please thank the staff for dinner. I mean to come again."

As she waved her off, Maree wished her sister a safe journey. She hoped she wasn't meeting Simon Markham on the way. She knew she shouldn't concern herself. After all Barbara at twenty-one ought to be capable of knowing what she was doing, but she also knew Simon for the brute he could be if he learned of their conversation. She prayed Barbara would say nothing about it. Hopefully she would be sensible and go to university.

Chapter 6

Young people were the topic of conversation when Maree arrived back in the dining room. It seemed Edith and Treve were happy just to sit where they were.

"I've ordered more coffee," Treve said.

They talked until Edith began to yawn.

"Time for bed," Maree smiled at Edith.

It was only as she was undressing that she felt the letter in her pocket. She sat on the bed to read it.

'Please don't forget your father's birthday, dear,' mother had written. 'We are planning a little surprise for him. One or two members of the church are dropping in. Aunt Sarah is making him a cake. I'm having a mini bake-up on Friday (he has two meetings at Dawlish so he'll be out of the way for a few hours). He will not have to work on Sat fourteenth though. We can give him a rousing birthday do. It would really make his day if you can be here. I hope Barbara remembers to give you this. Love Mum.

PS if you'd like to bring a couple of friends with you do so. No one is staying over. As you know, we have three unoccupied rooms beside yours."

Maree hadn't forgotten Dad's special day, but it seemed to have crept up on her much sooner than she'd expected. She hoped Edith would not want to set off for France before the fourteenth. Perhaps she'd do well to speak to Treve before Edith got to him. Edith would wait, she knew, but was she depriving her of an extra day of excitement?

A couple of weeks later, when Maree explained the dilemma, of course Matron had the answer.

"Simple," she said. "Take Edith with you."

"But what about you?" Maree protested. "We could be away for maybe three weeks when we go to France. It's hardly fair taking another weekend."

"You are removing the one misfit resident we have. Edith is a pet, but she does get into mischief. If she is not here I shall have less to do, and Treve won't be dropping in. Oh, don't get me wrong, I'm fond of them both, but if you are away then I'd sooner they were too. Now be off, remind me again a couple of weeks before the date."

In reception Maree found Treve fiddling with the plants. Startled on catching sight of her, he said, "Sorry, I couldn't resist nipping off a few dead leaves."

"I expect the gardener will appreciate it" she replied, "but I'm surprised to see you again so soon. I thought you were working for the next couple of weeks?"

"So did I, but the folk who required our exhibits sent some of their own staff to help select what they needed from our artefacts to save us the trouble. It meant we could close earlier than intended. My parents are anticipating elderly relatives to visit, so they have engaged a couple of extra hands to run the estate. I am surplus to requirements. I hoped you'd be pleased to see me."

"Oh, I am." His gaze became intense. Embarrassed, she asked, "Have you spoken to your aunt this morning?"

"No, but I spotted her reading a book on the seat in front of the oaks to the left. She looked so comfortable I left her there. Did you want her? I'll fetch her."

"Not necessary. I'd like to talk to you alone for a few minutes."

"Oh, that sounds ominous, what is it?"

"You remember you asked me to keep my eye on her for any odd behaviour patterns?"

"Yes, was I being over cautious?"

"No, it's just that she is being a little strange occasionally. The other afternoon we got a visit from the house next door. Apparently Edith was found in their garden, and when they welcomed her and enquired what they could do to help she said she was on her way to her room. She was escorted back here and the lady had a word with matron suggesting it wasn't the first time, so perhaps we should escort her and not let her go out alone. "

"Is that all?"

"A couple of times she's not been able to remember if she's eaten or is still waiting for her meal. Nothing much really to worry about, but..." Maree let it hang.

"Mm, well, not much to concern us, anyone can have a lapse of memory, but if it gets more frequent then we may have to persuade her to see a doctor. Perhaps I'll have a word with Matron later."

They walked down the drive and took the path toward the rear. On the way she told him of another afternoon when Edith had not got back from town until late. As before, he suggested she might have met a new friend and eaten out, so she had not required a meal on her return. It was strange that she had again offered no explanation and suggested maybe a tactful query might elicit something if it happened again. Maree hoped there would be no repeat.

Treve remarked on the work done on this portion of Oakland's grounds, saying "Parklands would have suited for a name just as well."

Maree agreed with him, though the flower-beds had not yet

fulfilled their early promise, for the summer flowers had barely begun to replace the withered spring bulbs.

"I know what you mean," she said. "And later on it will be even more beautiful." She sighed. "I remember how much I appreciated the peace and comfort of the whole garden when I first arrived. I've never lost the awe I felt then, or forgotten how much I needed it."

He took her arm. "I would like to hear more, but another time maybe, we have been spotted." Edith was waving, excitedly.

As they reached the seat Edith moved to the centre, indicating to Treve and Maree to sit either side of her. She thrust the book she had been perusing at Maree.

"Have you seen this?" she asked.

Maree took the book from her. Titled 'Theatrical Postcards,' its covers depicted prints of postcards copied from photographs of early twentieth-century stage artistes. She turned to Treve.

"Now you understand why your dear aunt did not see you earlier."

As she turned over the pages Treve said, "I'd like to look through it when we have more time. I take it this was before your era in the theatre, Aunt?"

Recalling why they were in the garden, Maree thought it was time to draw their attention to her query. She indicated the envelope.

"I've an invitation from my mother, which if you agree, would mean the three of us attending my father's birthday party on the fourteenth of July. What do you say? Would you like to accept? Matron is happy for us to go."

"Where do your parents live, Maree?"

"Dawlish in Devon. Dad has three churches in the Exeter diocese, and on special occasions that fall on a Saturday his curates take care of them."

"And Saturday fourteenth July is special occasion, no?" Edith laughed. "Oh, please I would like to attend, and Treve will drive us to... where did you say Maree?"

"Dawlish, it's only a few miles from Exeter. Perhaps we can leave there early on Sunday to take a stroll through the cathedral on our way home."

Treve smiled. Maree noted the mounting excitement on Edith's face while he thought about it.

"Yes, of course I will drive you, but I suggest it might be more convenient to take in the cathedral visit on Saturday morning. It means that to avoid rush hour traffic we must leave here early, possibly seven am." No need to ask if this suited Edith; her eyes sparkled.

The following days passed with a well-behaved Edith causing no inconvenience to either Matron or Maree. On Friday evening they loaded the car, which Treve left parked in Oaklands garage overnight. Saturday saw them away from the house with ten minutes to spare. Edith, as keyed up as a child, sat with Maree in the back and never stopped chattering, especially when Treve reminded her that as an eleven-year-old she had lived for a time at Teignmouth, which they would be travelling through.

It was a beautiful morning, the sky already blue and cloudless. Hedges coloured with wild flowers prompted in Edith the desire to stop and pick them for Maree's mother. Treve persuaded her to forget it in view of the distance they still had to travel. Something else causing her childish excitement were the wind farm turbines, which had sprung up on several locations since Maree had last travelled this route. Edith wanted to know if it was possible to go inside them and climb to the top.

"Make sure the seat belts are fastened properly," Treve whispered over his shoulder towards Maree. She smiled; the same thought must have crossed both his and Maree's minds not to let Edith out of the car.

They crossed the Tamar Bridge and rang Maree's home to let

her mother know they were now in Devon and would soon be with her. Later, parking at the end of the bridge separating Shaldon from Teignmouth, Treve took them for a short walk across the bridge. The tide was in and there was a view upriver of anglers in small boats fishing, while many others tried their luck along the banks of the Teign. The scene contrasted with the larger cargo ships anchored in the harbour facing the estuary. One ship had run aground on the central mound of accumulated silt known locally as the Salty, causing great excitement among the visitors and children.

They were more than halfway across the bridge towards Shaldon when Treve laid his hand on Maree's arm. Drawing her close, he pointed out a narrow, steep hill facing them.

"I want to show you something" he said. He pulled an envelope from his pocket and taking a snapshot from it, called Edith to come close. "Do you recognise this?"

Edith tried to take it from him, but he held it tightly.

"No you cannot have it, I want Maree to see what a naughty girl you were at eleven years old."

"May I?" Maree asked. Treve handed it to her. A small girl, hair in pigtails, one ribbon missing, skirt tucked inside dark-coloured knickers, was in the act of climbing a tree. A ladder was propped against a similar tree. A couple of bicycles lay on the ground.

"Is this someone I should know?" Maree asked. Treve nodded toward Edith, who was giggling.

"So why didn't you use the ladder to scale the tree?"

"How can I climb and show the boys I am as good as they if I can only do it from a ladder?" Edith asked.

"And I can tell you that on one occasion she ended up in the river," Treve said.

"Oh no, how did you manage that?" Maree laughed. Edith shook her head as though she'd forgotten.

"At the far end of this bridge on your right there used to be camping pitches for a dozen or so tents," Treve said. "This particular weekend there were very few tents in the field. Someone had removed the fencing so the side facing the river had no barrier. Edith had come down that steep hill on her bicycle, being chased by the owner of a local orchard on his. Slowing to turn in off the road her brakes failed. Crossing the field the bike hit a submerged rock and flew through the air, landing in the centre of the river. My precious aunt was left sitting where she landed, on the mud bank."

"Well, obviously someone fished her out before it was too late." Maree looked at Edith fondly. "So she wasn't in too much danger."

Treve placed an arm around his aunt's shoulders. "Actually she did quite well out of it. The man who'd removed that bit of fencing to get his newly-painted boat into the water pulled her out of the mud, then took her round the corner to buy a new bicycle. Someone did eventually get the damaged one out of the mud, but it was useless, it could never have been ridden again."

"And I did not tell him the brakes had not worked successfully for a long, long time before that day," Edith said.

"Perhaps I'm not being fair" Treve said. "I wasn't even around at the time, this is one of the little tales I gleaned from my mother." He handed the photo to Edith. "I think you are old enough to have this as a keepsake now." Edith put it carefully into her handbag.

"A visitor took that photo and sent it to the cycle shop" said Treve. "The proprietor passed it on to Edith's mother. My mother found it in a drawer."

Maree thought it surprising Edith's mother had kept it.

As they strolled back the way they had come and up the slight incline that was the Teignmouth road, Edith pointed to another steep hill on the left.

"I remember that one. We could scoot down it. There wasn't so much traffic then. People walked as though they might be expecting a girl on a bicycle to come down very fast, and another strange thing Maree, they have a hospital at the top. Sick people should not have to climb such hills for treatment."

Back in the car it was agreed they were early enough to spend a while sitting on the promenade at Teignmouth to watch the railway trains emerge from the tunnel on their journey to Penzance. Once the novelty of the first trains had worn off Edith was particularly quiet. Maree wondered how many facets of her character were there. At times she could be, exuberant, mischievous and childishly teasing, at others truculent and sulky, with a hard exterior. Now, quiet and withdrawn, she was the gentle ladylike Edith Maree knew existed but seldom saw.

The service and food were excellent in the small, comfortable restaurant. Maree had dined there on numerous days off from duties at the vicarage. They were in before the lunchtime rush, having told Maree's mother they would do their best to arrive by 2 pm. Walking had given them all good appetites, and they ate heartily.

Edith, who always enjoyed her food, kept glancing around, her blue eyes darting here and there taking in the décor, the pictures on the walls, the richly-decorated ceiling and, surreptitiously, the other diners. Maree realised this was a treat for her.

It seemed to Maree that since she herself had arrived at Oaklands, Edith had had very little opportunity of going out for simple pleasure. There were visits to the hairdresser, and occasional sorties to the larger fashion shops to purchase a special garment. There were days when residents went off by coach on all-day excursions, but Edith didn't always join them. That was about it. To see her enjoying this trip was gratifying.

Before leaving the restaurant Treve produced his map, now he was in unknown territory.

"According to my timetable we should be at Exeter Cathedral in thirty minutes," he announced. "If we spend another thirty minutes visiting we can make it to your home in approximately one hour and a half, Maree."

"Thank you Treve. Mother is inclined to worry if guests are late arriving when travelling any distance, and today being Dad's day we do not want to give them any cause for extra concern."

"Is your father a pious man, Maree? Will he not like us to have fun when we are all together?"

Maree hoped Edith's question was not the prelude to mischief she was planning. "Of course he will want you to have fun, Edith. Anyway today is his day off, he'll want to have fun himself."

Exeter Cathedral is beautiful. No doubt the majority of its visitors go straight inside, but Edith had to go darting off. Treve and Maree followed. When they finally caught up with her she explained.

"When we came in I heard a lady say to someone that we must not go until we've seen the West Front. So I come to see. Please can you tell me how could someone carve all those figures?"

Treve took her arm, "Please Aunt, stay with us. We must go around fairly quickly or we shall not see half of it." The choir was not in evidence but an organist began playing 'Amazing Grace.'

"Is there anything particular you'd like to see, Edith?" Maree asked.

"Everything is particular." Edith's voice had grown quiet. She was evidently overawed by the majesty all around her.

"We will get you an official guide book, Aunt," Treve promised, "then you will have a souvenir as well as something to study when we get back to Oaklands. Who knows, maybe one day you can come to Exeter again and you will know what to look for."

Maree had been before, but she too would have liked to spend more time there. The day being warm, it was a great temptation to remain outside, but she was especially interested in the Great East Window. The literature stated that it was Exeter's finest stained glass from the 14th century. It enthralled her. She spent far too long gazing at it and was quite startled when Treve placed an arm around her shoulders whispering they should make their way to the exit.

"You had better go to the shop to buy Edith's guide book. I'll keep my eye on her," she advised Treve. They didn't need to be in that much of a hurry, but she did not want to encourage Edith to dawdle, or cause her mother any anxiety.

Chapter 7

At the Vicarage, Maree's parents' home, Barbara was waiting for them, standing close to Simon's bright red Jaguar, which was parked at the bottom of the steps leading to the front door.

"I'm so glad you're not late," Barbara said, smiling. "Mother has taken Dad out to the kitchen garden at the back. He doesn't know you are coming and she was beginning to despair of keeping him occupied until you arrived. The two aunts are preparing things in the kitchen. One of them will slip out to signal mum once you're inside."

Barbara seemed pleased to see Treve and Edith again, greeting them both with a kiss. "Do come in. Once you have seen Mum and Dad I'll show you to your rooms."

"A beautiful house," Edith murmured to Maree. "You were lucky to grow up in such English surroundings. It is from Victorian period, yes?"

Maree nodded. "Yes, thank you, Edith, we all enjoy living here."

Entering the large, gracefully-furnished drawing room, Edith followed her remark with a loud "Ooh!" of approval. Treve too gazed around in wonder. He managed to whisper, "It's beautiful, Maree."

She looked for her parents. At last, there they were, the two people in the world most dear to her. Introductions over, she prepared herself for their embraces. Smiling as always, Dad appeared not to have lost any of his six feet in height, or any hair, which, though it was now silver grey, for a sixty-year-old was thick and luxuriant. He hugged her as though she had been away for ten years. Mother's eyes were full of tears. As they exchanged hugs she whispered, "He didn't guess it would be you, although he did keep asking who all the food was for. Thank you dear. I'm so glad you are staying over. We can have a long talk after breakfast tomorrow."

She raised her voice. "Welcome, all of you, and thank you for coming. Now who wants tea or coffee? It will be ready when you come down after Barbara has shown you your rooms."

Maree was in her old room, and for a few minutes she stood with her back against the door looking around. When she had come home from the training hospital, qualified but unable to obtain a nursing post anywhere in the West Country, she'd decided to work for her father until something turned up, and this room was one of the reasons why. Even now she could not look at the large wooden bed without her mind returning to her childhood. In turn the bed had become a nest where she and Barbara had pretended it would protect them from all kinds of dangers, a curtained four-poster where they were beautiful princesses waiting to be rescued by handsome princes, and later, as teenagers, an eastern divan, where they reclined to read exotic literature and consume large quantities of Turkish delight.

Photographs of them as children stood on the cabinets either side of the bed. She had begged her mother to update them, but she'd refused. They were her links with the past, she insisted.

An armchair covered in chintz stood invitingly in the large bay window. An ottoman, its lid covered in the same material, remained as it always had, standing at the foot of the bed. At the windows pale cream curtains with sprays of summer flowers were drawn back with ties. On the magnolia-coloured walls were framed prints of Dartmoor.

The time she'd been away she'd missed this room, the building and her family. Staying and working here had been an easy option. She'd never wanted to go away again. Sighing, she shook her head. She had become disillusioned at not being able to arrange time for herself. When working for Dad he'd expected her to be available precisely when he needed. She had been more tired than if she'd been working nine to five for a business in the nearby city of Exeter. Mum understood. Whether she ever mentioned it to Dad, Maree had no idea.

One day he had arrived home with a visitor, the family solicitor.

"This is Simon Markham. Simon, Maree, my daughter." Simon took her hand.

"So like your lovely wife," he said to her father before turning to look deeply into her eyes. "And how long are you intending to stay in this neck of the woods? Forever I hope," he added quietly, voice low.

"Maree is working for me, Simon. Until she gets tired of us."

"Dad!" she protested. "Please don't say that, as if I could ever get tired of you or Mum."

And it could have stayed like that, if she had not been foolish enough to get engaged to Simon. At first everything was fine. Then Simon began to find fault with the hours she worked. Although they had never discussed finance, he decided that she wasn't being paid the rate for the job, that her father didn't know but should be made aware that the wage book he consulted was out of date and that he, Simon, would make enquiries and inform her father of his errors.

She had disagreed strongly, telling him it was none of his business. It wasn't their first argument. She was beginning to realise she had made a serious mistake. Dad took it in good part. He didn't query how Simon knew about her wages. He made it plain that if he really was underpaying her then he had to be corrected, that Simon was only looking after his future wife.

Mother agreed; she thought Maree was making a fuss about nothing and should be grateful that Simon, busy as he was with his father's business, still found time to look after her interests.

They had no idea how much time Simon spent at the leisure club on the pretext of looking into his father's clients' business. He had also started to bully her. When she discovered him searching through her father's private family papers and he could offer no legitimate reason for doing so, they had rowed. Maree had returned the engagement ring, telling him to leave the house and not come back.

He had come visiting her parents again. What explanation he'd offered her father she had no idea. Mother, though annoyed with what she saw as a lack of manners in someone else's home, didn't think it was bad enough for Maree to break off the engagement. "He was almost family!" she had said, as though that was all the permission he needed.

When Maree entered the drawing room now, Simon was among the guests. For what could only have been seconds they looked at each other. Maree felt nothing. It was definitely over. She made up her mind to ignore him from then on. Barbara came in carrying the tray of drinks and placed it on the large ornate sideboard. Handing the drinks around, she had a cheery word with everyone.

The afternoon started off well, with one and all wishing her father the happiest of birthdays. Though there were enough chairs for all, Maree managed to sit between her parents. Barbara sat between Simon and Treve. Once or twice during the afternoon of busy chatter she saw her father casting puzzled glances in Edith's direction; she wondered why.

Once the delicious tea and the cake cutting were over Edith gave the birthday man a present, a beautiful Paisley scarf, informing him it was for the occasions when he had to remove his doggie collar. It would protect his precious throat and his wife would have to find somewhere else to attach his lead. Hilarious laughter greeted the remark.

Early in the evening, the local guests began to leave. Not having to make the long journey back to Oaklands, Edith and Maree retired to their rooms to change into something comfortable to sit around in.

"I'll see you presently," Edith said as they parted outside Maree's room.

Maree changed her dress for a cool and comfortable sleeveless one and repaired her makeup. Taking off her court shoes, she slipped into a pair of casuals. She was putting a comb through her hair when there came a brisk knock on her door. Opening it, expecting it to be Edith, she was startled to find Simon. Stepping quickly inside, he pulled the door from her hand, shutting it firmly behind him. He took a menacing step toward her.

"I need to talk to you."

"But I have no wish to talk to you." Maree stepped backwards, but not far enough. She was still within reach, and he grabbed her arm with both hands. Too late, she recalled his trick of twisting the skin above the wrist one way, and below in the opposite direction. Later in their relationship Maree had learned it was known as a Chinese burn. It had been a favourite cruelty of his whenever she'd been slow to jump to his orders, and as always it brought tears to her eyes. She hit out with her other hand, catching him full on the side of his face. Too late, she realised she was still holding the comb. Blood was already oozing from the scratches. He released her wrist immediately.

"Oh, Daddy's girl is fighting back," he sneered as he put his hand to his wounded cheek. "You'll pay dearly for that." He pulled a handkerchief from his pocket, dabbing at the area. Another knock on the door forced him to turn away as Maree stepped forward to open it and admit Barbara.

"Oh, I see! Secret assignations?" Barbara grinned at her sister. "Mum is wondering where you two are. I don't think she imagined for a minute you were together. Interesting I must say." She smiled at Maree. She looked at Simon, "So, what are you doing in Maree's room? I don't imagine you were invited." Simon ignored her. "None of your business," he said, and left the room.

"You ready?" Barbara asked her sister.

Maree nodded and opened her wardrobe, taking out a cardigan to hide the injury. Her wrist was already hurting. She knew it would soon begin to turn blue and the bruise would be clearly visible on her fair skin.

When the sisters returned downstairs it was to find that their father and Treve had deserted them. Edith arrived behind them.

"I know where they've gone," their mother said. "Come with me."

After they had followed her into the kitchen garden, they discovered the two men at the far end leaning on the five-barred gate that gave access into the lane leading to the church lychgate. "We thought you might enjoy a walk," Dad said.

Edith and their mother walked together. Treve and Barbara paired off. This left Dad and Maree. The two aunts declined to walk, preferring to sit on the first bench they came to.

"They have worked hard most of the day preparing for the party" Dad said. "They deserve their time of rest". Mother and Edith were giggling like a couple of schoolgirls as they set off together.

"Any idea where Edith hails from originally?" Dad asked Maree.

"She is English. I believe she was born here in Devon. Why do you ask?"

"Did you see that lovely scarf she gave me for my birthday? I've always admired those on other people, I'm delighted to have one of my own."

"A glimpse only Dad, there was so much going on at that time."

"Well," he said, pulling the scarf from his pocket, "Simon thought it looked expensive. He was interested in it so I looked at the label and discovered it had been made in France."

"Every possibility that's where she bought it," Maree said. "Edith spent many years in France. In fact she married a French cartographer. He was killed some years ago."

"I must have a word with her" Dad said, returning the scarf to his pocket. "I feel sure we've met before, but for the life of me I can't think where."

"She was in France until three years ago," Maree told him, "so unless you can claim the same I'm afraid you must be mistaken."

"I'll find a few moments between now and your leaving tomorrow. It will plague me no end if I don't at least ask her. I can't believe I could forget those eyes."

"They are lovely," she said, "and you're seeing them at their best today."

Dad laughed. "I can imagine them full of mischief."

She smiled. "Edith knows all about mischief."

"I have a book in the study describing character and features," said her father. "The chapter on eyes claims that eyes like hers, small and deeply set, denote a love of intrigue, and because they are bright blue and wide open, elegance, taste, discrimination in all matters connected with the arts, self-respect etc, point out a laughing personality. I'm sure there was a song associated with her name."

"Were you ever in France Dad?" Maree couldn't remember him mentioning it, but he had spent some time working overseas before he had found himself drawn to the Anglican ministry. That had been several years ago. She knew he had been in two or three parishes in Devon before coming to Dawlish, but her own serious studies into nursing had taken over before she could spend time enquiring further into her father's career.

"As a matter of fact I lived in France as a student," he said. "I was in my late twenties. I came home to England for a holiday, the best holiday of my life, for I met your mother and decided not to return to France. I was able to continue my studies at a university here in England although it was hard work persuading your mother that I was doing the right thing career wise."

"What were you studying?"

"Theology in my early years in France. I delved into a lot of 'ologies', but it was difficult to find one that pointed me in a definite direction. I felt I was being guided toward the church, but it was a while before my studies into the Anglican ministry satisfied my youthful ideals." He nodded thoughtfully. "I was full of zeal in those days."

"Then you could have met Edith in France. She was sent to a finishing school in Lyon when she was only fifteen."

"Ah now, you may have something there, but wait a minute, on second thoughts, unless she went on to a university later I doubt our paths would have crossed."

But Maree felt her father was on the right track. He seemed so sure he'd met Edith before. She wanted him to be right. She knew that if he jogged Edith's memory she would come up with something.

With frequent stops to look at the wild flowers and recently planted shrubs, they continued until her mother and Edith indicated they were returning to the house. When Maree and her father caught up with them they were already seated in the conservatory. Mother asked to be excused, leaving Edith to Maree. Knowing her father's intentions, Maree also made a discreet exit.

She felt certain he would not want her clouding the issue.

When she returned later they were deep in conversation. From Edith's excited expression as she rose and came toward her, Maree was sure they had discovered a mutual topic.

"Oh Maree!" she said, clasping her friend's hand, "I am so pleased you bring me to your parent's home. Your father and me have shared some memories of my beloved France."

Her father too came to join them.

"It's true Maree, Edith spent some years on the stage in France. She tells me she was playing in comedy at the Variety Theatre to begin with, that will be where I first saw her." He placed his arm fondly around Edith's shoulders. "I missed the Gilbert and Sullivan operettas I regularly sang in before I left England, then when I was in France someone directed me to the Variety."

"And are you telling me Edith was playing there?"

"No," her father said, "Edith was in the audience. She was resting between plays. We had seats next to each other. In the interval we introduced ourselves. Edith was excited to discover I too was English." Edith was nodding in agreement. "Tonight I have excited her again, finding out that I was the young Englishman she met all those years ago."

Treve and Barbara arrived. "That is an ideal walk," Treve said. "Pity you missed it Maree."

Edith laughed, tapping his hand. "But you forget Treve, Maree and her father live here for many years. They will know all the walks in this part of the country." She turned to Maree. "Your father is a charming man." Laughingly, she delved into her handbag. "Now I have a request to you all."

Like magic a camera appeared, and she deftly handed it to Maree's father. "Please to take photographs of us," she said. Turning quickly to link arms with Simon, who had just entered the room, and Treve, she walked them to the sofa.

"We will sit together."

" Oh no!" Simon struggled to release himself from her grasp. "I dislike having snaps taken." But Edith held on.

"Be a good boy, Simon, I want pictures to remind me of such a happy time with this lovely family."

Simon continued to protest, and he was careful to present the non-injured cheek to the camera before reluctantly giving in. Treve, aware that his aunt was enjoying this day, gave no trouble. With the first shot completed by Dad, Treve was instructed to take one of Edith, first with Simon on his own and then with each individual with her, the exception being Mum and Dad. Here she wanted to sit between them. Then Treve took another of them as the loving couple they were.

Photography session over and camera safely stowed away in Edith's handbag, Maree sat beside her.

"So have you caught up with what has happened to you and Dad over the years?"

Maree knew they could not possibly have exchanged much information. Then she noticed her father making his way out of the conservatory.

"I would like your father to come to visit us at Truro, then we will have much time to talk," replied Edith. You must arrange it before we leave here tomorrow."

"Yes," Maree said thoughtfully, " but won't it be easier if we wait until this French trip is over? Maybe we can invite them both down to stay at the Cranwell for a short holiday. You can be their guide if I'm working. They'll take you out in the car."

" Oh Maree, you are in the right place of work that is also good for me to live there."

Her eyes lit up, revealing the quick, laughing personality the Oaklands staff so often saw in her. She took Maree's hand. "I do not understand why you have no gentlemen friends. They are not sensible, the English men. They cannot see the wood for the forest in front of their eyes." She spread her arms wide, shrugging her narrow shoulders, adding. "No matter, the handsome French men will not look over your charms, you will see." She laughed. "But I must be sure to bring you back to Oaklands, your father will be most displeased if I leave you behind in France."

Simon, though sharing the small settee with Barbara, was looking in their direction. How much of Edith's speech had he heard? Thankfully her mother was called out by one of the aunts. Edith immediately chose to sit next to her father, leaving Treve alone. He held out his hand, indicating the seat beside him. Maree took it, surprised to discover she'd missed him while walking with Dad but consoled herself with the thought she would be sharing him only with Edith tomorrow.

"This has been a very special day for you too, hasn't it Maree? Has it lived up to expectations?"

"Oh yes, more so," Maree said, making herself comfortable. "I've always loved my home and family, now that I can come back whenever I wish I'm less reluctant to leave. But it is thanks to you this time Treve." Treve shook his head. She continued, "You drove. Yes I know I have a car, but it's not as up to date as some and I'm not as competent a driver as you. We would have got here, but a few hours after the deadline."

Treve laughed, "As long as you did get here that's all that matters."

"Now," She said, changing the subject "did you know that my Father and Edith had met many years ago?"

"No!" He was, as expected, surprised. " How did that come about?"

"Apparently they met in France."

At that moment Barbara rose and went out.

"Come and sit with me, Edith." Simon's voice had always managed to make a request sound like an order. Edith, with a murmured "Excuse me" to Dad, immediately changed seats.

"But that is quite extraordinary Maree, where?"

"Dad says in the Variety Theatre. I've yet to hear Edith's side of the story. I think we'd better leave it until the journey back to Oaklands tomorrow. Tonight Edith is as excited as I've ever seen her. She will be calmer then."

"You are probably right, Maree. I've been watching her since we arrived here, she is a changed woman, so relaxed and happy."

Simon's voice carried across to them. "Tell me, Edith, how often do you visit France?"

His question brought only a quiet response from Edith, which in turn, had an effect on Simon, for the conversation was low key from then on.

Later Maree heard him say, "Come into the conservatory". Again Edith rose obediently and followed him.

After supper, though none of them were hungry enough to eat much, Edith came to say she wanted Simon to join them on the journey to France. She reasoned that as a solicitor he could speak to his French equivalent about the property still awaiting settlement. He would also, she said, be another voice to enquire about her fans. This was topped off with the assurance that he could also help with the driving, thereby giving Treve a rest.

Maree decided she would have a few words with her father. She couldn't face the thought of travelling several miles with her ex-fiancée's face grimacing at her from the rear view mirror.

Treve, who had no idea that Simon and Maree were once engaged to be married, asked quietly, "Who the blazes does Markham think he is? Doesn't he realise the car is mine? If I require assistance I'll find my own, I will not have someone I don't know take charge of my vehicle especially in a country where driving can be difficult, and it will be carrying precious passengers."

"This is partly my fault, Treve," Maree whispered. "Let me have a word with Dad, I'm sure he'll come up with a solution."

Treve's reply was to grab her hand and haul her gently to her feet. "Come on, let's go for a walk, it's still light enough to see our way through the garden."

Once outside he headed for the summerhouse, where the cushioned seats were warm from the earlier sun. Here they could have a conversation in comfort without being overheard.

Treve's first words surprised her. "Now what's all this about Markham's suggestion being brought about by you?"

"That wasn't what I meant, Treve." Maree managed to get the next words out without stumbling over them. "I was once engaged to him. Now there's a possibility I might be going to France he probably thinks that if he can get close again I will want him to come with me. He's been trying to patch things up by visiting Oaklands frequently. He's become quite close to Edith." She shrugged. "I believe that, knowing she and I are friends, he hopes to talk her into persuading me. I don't suppose Edith has told him she's paying for it."

"Oh I see, the chance of a holiday at your expense?"

"I don't know about that. He's a fee earner, he should be able to take himself to France."

"Then it must be you he wants. I'm afraid it's too late Maree, I want us to be more than friends, and I have a closer relationship with Aunt Edith than he can ever have. Now tell me, do I stand any chance?"

He rose from his seat, pulling Maree from hers and drawing her close. In his arms she felt secure and at ease. She glanced up as he bent his head to kiss her, his lips gentle. She wasn't sure what her own feelings were toward him; she'd lived to regret her last venture into romance.

"I like you, Treve." She smiled up at him. "But I need more time."

"As with other treasure, I can wait." He murmured against her hair.

When they returned Simon was not in evidence. The radio had been switched on. The nine o'clock news came to an end, and a musical programme followed. Soon they were aware of two sweet voices, Maree's mother and Edith, accompanying the music of the Gilbert and Sullivan Operetta 'Iolanthe'. To her further surprise her father joined in, taking the part of Strephon. Though this was a young man's role his voice was as strong and true as it had always been. What a wonderful weekend this was turning out to be.

Chapter 8

Maree rose early next morning. Her arm above the wrist having developed a bruise as she'd expected, a cardigan was again necessary. She hoped no one would notice and draw attention to it.

She found her father strolling among the shrubbery in the garden. He did no gardening on Sundays, as with two services in churches a few miles apart he didn't risk wasting time doing anything but prepare for them.

"Well my lovely daughter, it seems we are the only early risers in the house this bright and beautiful morning."

"Good morning, Dad. Can we sit in the summerhouse? I have a favour to ask."

"Of course dear. I take it you wish to be private?"

She smiled at him as they settled. "It is lovely here, you have made it so comfortable."

"Thank you dear. Now before we are interrupted you had better tell me what it is you require my help with."

Maree explained the situation. Her father agreed that it could become difficult and said he'd speak to Simon as soon as possible.

"He's a reasonable man. I'm sure he'll see how awkward it

could be for all of you. He can, of course make his own way to France. I could have no influence on him then."

"I'm sure you will know just the right words to use, Dad, whereas I should end up arguing with him. Edith thinks he's a dreamboat and she seems to want him to join us. I couldn't bring myself to tell her of the past. If she thought Simon was hankering after starting it all up again, out would come her match making skills I'm sure."

As if she knew she was the subject of their conversation, Edith came trotting along the garden path with a purposeful air straight to the summerhouse. She showed no surprise at seeing them. Her "good morning" was cheerful, followed by, "I guessed you would be here early, if only for a little peace before you are to preach to your parishioners."

Dad rose, putting his arm across her shoulders. "I'm afraid you are a little late if you wanted to talk to me. I am to have my breakfast in the next ten minutes, half an hour after that I must be on my way."

"What time will you return to the house?" Edith asked. "I have a small surprise for you before we leave."

"If no one wishes to speak with me at length after the service I will return about ten thirty."

"That will be good." They moved off together leaving Maree to follow, wondering what Edith's small surprise was?

Barbara, Edith and Treve accompanied Maree's father to morning service. Maree remained behind helping her mother prepare lunch, and when everything was ready they placed it in the oven, taking their coffee into the conservatory.

"What do you think of Barbara's attraction to Simon?"

Maree couldn't tell from her mother's voice if she was happy about it.

"I hope it doesn't come to anything serious," Maree said. "At her age she should finish her education. I'm hoping she takes the opportunity to go to Leeds."

Her mother sighed. "She is wavering right now, and not as determined as she was a few months ago. Your proposed trip to France has made her think again."

"Oh, why?"

"She hasn't said anything definite, but I feel that while she remains here working for Dad she has Simon breathing down her neck telling her what to do. I'm sure it's beginning to rankle, as he still does as he pleases and goes where he wants."

"What does Dad think? He will have to look around for another secretary if she does go to university."

"Your father's had a tentative word regarding what she can do with her life in years to come if she has the right education now. I'm sure he's thought it all through and, as with your education, he wants only what's best for her."

"Once she settles in at a university she'll wonder why she ever had doubts," Maree said. "Of course she'll have quite a lot of studying, so hopefully she won't have time to worry about my French trip. All things being equal she'll meet up with a young man her own age."

Their mother's Sunday lunches were without parallel in the family, and they did this one justice. Edith's surprise, when delivered, turned out to be a well-drawn, well-written invitation to Mr and Mrs Bolitho to visit Oaklands, possibly in the late autumn or at a time of their choosing.

Edith had been quiet on arrival at Maree's parents' home. She was even quieter when it was time to leave. Everyone was a little sad, but amidst promises to come again soon they left. No reference to France was made when saying goodbye. Simon did not appear. Maree presumed he'd gone to his own home the night before.

They stopped on Bodmin Moor for a picnic, which had been given to Treve to stow in the boot. Edith loved the moor. She wanted to explore, especially the areas around the old silver mining ruins and the granite quarries she could see in the distance. When Maree explained that they were much like other mines in Cornwall, it made her even more eager. Treve promised that before the winter set in they would travel up again and see them. She talked of nothing else all the way home.

They were almost back at Oaklands when Maree realised there'd been no mention of the stage or a look at the book of postcard replicas.

"One day you must both come for afternoon tea, then I will talk of Theatre Comedy and my time with them," Edith promised them.

In the meantime Maree thought she should check up on the Truro Players group. Having heard Edith's sweet singing voice, Maree was sure she could still be of use to a talented group.

Nothing seemed to have changed at Oaklands. Treve unloaded the car, stayed long enough for a bite to eat and assuring them before he left he would see them the next day. Maree called at the office, where Matron was pleased they'd returned safely. Mark, checking security, had discovered the interior storeroom lock broken. The place was a shambles. It had been thoroughly gone over.

"Which means that someone other than those of us with keys had been in there. I wonder what they were looking for?" Maree said.

"Normally it contains nothing of any value," Matron said, "so this time I accompanied Mark. I was shocked to see what damage could be done under our very noses and we'd heard nothing."

"What have you done about it?" Maree was sure Matron would not have let the matter rest without trying to do something.

"We called the police and of course I felt compelled to tell them of Edith's missing fans, though I can't be sure it has anything to do with the break-in. One of the officers seems to know a great deal about the value of antiques, including fans." She sighed. "Apparently they have a list of items that have gone missing in the last year or so. He has promised to come and talk to Edith hoping that between them they can come up with an estimated value if she can describe them."

"When will you tell her?"

"I'll save it until the morning, she is probably tired tonight. Now tell me how the weekend went."

They talked for an hour. When Maree finally got into bed she didn't know if she should be glad or sorry the French trip might be off.

The young constable spent a couple of hours with Edith the following morning; she told Maree later that he seemed to think she had let someone in to see the store.

"I told him I had no key and it would have made no difference if I had shown someone where the store was. If they had no key they could not get in."

"So what is he going to do about it?" Maree asked.

"He wants pictures of the fans he can show to his superiors."

"Can you remember what they looked like?"

"I can do better, I have photographs."

"But that's wonderful, Edith. Are the fans insured?"

"Yes, they are valuable. I must insure or the removing company would not carry them to England."

"You were going to put them on display weren't you?"

"Some time when there is more room I would have liked to display. But now I think I should get finished with them. Give them to a theatre company who would make use of them." She shook her head. "It makes no sense to keep them out of sight all the time in case they are stolen."

"But they are your memories of your time on the French stage. How would anyone know about them?"

Edith shrugged her shoulders, looking at Maree with a puzzled frown.

"I do not know, maybe I talk too much to somebody."

"But who?" Maree queried, "You don't have many visitors,

and," she added gently, "you promised to show them to me. I've never seen them, so I take it you have never had them out on view. If that's the case, how could anyone know they were in the store to steal?"

"Oh, Maree, you are like policeman, you ask so many questions which I cannot answer."

"When is the policeman coming back to see the photographs?"

"I have to go to the police station this afternoon, if you can take me. The photos were hidden too, so I was unable to show him when he was here with me."

"Maybe Treve will take you, he said he may call today."

" I promise to go at two o'clock. Maybe Treve will not be here by that time."

"If Treve doesn't come by one-thirty then I will take you. I've promised to take another resident to the hairdresser's. Can you remember when you last saw your fans?"

"I have been thinking very carefully since we talked before. I am sure it was here in my room. Simon had come to see me. I did not show them to him because he came too late and I had put them away. He was much interested in my theatre photographs and one of me with my bicycle. He said I should go out cycling now. It was good for people to exercise. He is very fit man, he tells me. I did not speak of my exercises. They would have been only little compared to what he was telling me he did."

"Oh, Edith, I think you would have to be very careful, the roads are much more dangerous than when you cycled as a girl." What had Simon been thinking of, Maree wondered?

"Pouf!" she exclaimed. "I will not be able to go anywhere soon, for the big lorries do not see little cyclists or walkers. They will knock me over and then laugh at me. When you are engaged in your work I will walk to the shops, or when Treve visits I will ask him to take me."

"So, Edith, to get back to your fans, you are saying they were never in the inside store, but in your room the whole time."

73

"True, Matron added two and two and made five I think."

"Then I wonder why someone broke into the store. There was nothing in there except empty trunks and cases."

"I say to you before, maybe I talk too much. Someone might have thought I would put my cabinet of fans in there for safe keeping while I am away to your home in Dawlish. Do you not think I am right?"

"Probably you are. Now all you have to do is remember who you said it to, then we can tell the policeman this afternoon and he can start searching for this person."

"You think well, Maree, but I do not know if I will remember so easily. Lots of things have happened to me since then."

She avoided looking at Maree. Maree felt Edith was not telling her the whole truth, but why? They were her fans. If she wanted to see them again, her best chance was by telling the truth to the police.

Maree squeezed Edith's shoulder. "I must go to work now. If Treve does not come by lunchtime, I will come and see you. Meanwhile, you had better get the photographs out and put them safely in your handbag."

Maree talked the whole thing over with Matron, and they came to the conclusion that Edith had remembered who she had talked to but did not want to put that person to any inconvenience. They could think of nobody other than Treve or Simon who she knew well enough to take to her room. They had never seen the fans, so were in no position to assess their value.

Treve did not arrive before lunch. As she'd promised, Maree took Edith to the police station after dropping the other resident, who did not need taking back to Oaklands, off at the hairdresser's, wishing instead to return in her own time.

The constable was ready for them. They were taken to a room which was possibly used for interviews. After showing them to a couple of chairs pulled from under the table, the officer opened a large folder, and for the next hour they compared like for like, discussing some of the history. Intrigued by Edith's photographs, he was, he said, eager and hopeful of seeing the real articles in the not too distant future.

"You are probably wondering at my interest," he commented.

Edith nodded happily. "I should like to know how you get such information. It is not from books, is it?"

"No, at least not at present, but many years ago when I was learning cabinet-making I made a hand fan for my sister who was to act in a school play. I spent many hours poring over the intricacies of the fans from many countries."

Maree herself was fascinated. The fans were, for the most part, beautiful works of art. She could see why someone would have thought they were worth stealing. Because of their uniqueness the policeman thought they would be difficult to sell on the open market. He promised to visit all the local auction salerooms and make the salesmen aware that they could be dealing with stolen property if they offered fans for sale without consulting the list he gave them. They were both surprised when he promised that all auction salerooms, antique shops and second-hand shops in the country would be informed.

"Well Mrs Arneau, you have certainly opened my eyes," he said. "I had no idea that anyone in Truro kept such lovely works of art in their home. Which of all these do you consider the most valuable?"

"Are you asking me which I value most or which would fetch most money on the open market?" asked Edith. Maree was surprised at her query.

"On the market," he replied.

"That is not difficult. The one which would fetch most money at market is this one." She offered him a photograph. "It is believed to be German, about 1700-1710. It is called a découpé fan."

"I'm not sure I have the details of that, Mrs Arneau. Perhaps while I check you can be selecting the one which means most to you."

Edith sorted through, selecting a picture of a fan that appeared to be made entirely of lace. "This, I am sure, is French," she said, offering it to him.

He turned it over and read aloud: "Folding fan with hand-coloured lithograph, probably French, circa 1850-60".

"But this is my greatest favourite. When I played the daughter of a wealthy Chinese business family, this one never left my hand the whole time I was on stage. It is known as the Leaf. This is the one I am most sad at losing. Please, anything you can do about recovering it, please do it."

He took the photograph, entitled "The Braganza Fan," and read. "Chinese, The Leaf, circa 1808. It is lovely. These Chinese ladies are beautifully dressed and they would not be completely attired without their fans."

"I can see why this is a special favourite," Maree said, taking it from the policeman. "So many of them are old, Edith, where did you get them? They must have cost you a lot of money."

"Sometimes I act in plays which needed fans, maybe the stage property box would have only damaged ones which I would be able to repair, or we would go into the market house in Strasbourg and buy what we could find there. Occasionally one of the members would be leaving our troupe and decline to carry her fans with her. Those of us left behind purchased them for a few francs only. Many of us bargained for the beautiful ones, and often I was the most lucky, so, I make it my business to buy a case to fit them all in."

"They are all beautiful, Edith," Maree assured her as the policeman tapped in the details on his laptop. A few minutes later he rose, extending his hand to Edith. "You may leave it with me now, Mrs Arneau. Rest assured I will do my utmost to trace your fans and I will be in touch as soon as there is anything to report." He shook hands with Maree, who thanked him for his efforts.

As they set off back to the car Maree asked, "How big is the case? Edith, is it heavy to carry?"

"No Maree, it is like a small attaché case, not at all heavy, the fans are of no weight."

"I'm sure Matron would appreciate being shown them. Perhaps you will both come to my room, we will have afternoon tea. You can explain the background of those you know about. The others we could make a list of and we can go to the library and study books like your theatrical postcards are in. We can also look for fans in France, if we are still going there."

"That will be a good idea, Maree. But I am sorry to say there will be a sad lack of them in France. It is many years since fans have been on display or for sale. Other countries such as Spain still make them but not of the same quality." She looked enquiringly at her friend.

"You have never been to France, Maree?"

Maree shook her head. "No, I was very much looking forward to my first visit with Treve and you. How long will we be staying?"

"I will think about it and then speak to Matron. She too will need a holiday, so we must consider her. Perhaps we have one holiday soon. If we find what we look for quickly then maybe we go back to Oaklands. When matron has returned from her holiday we can go somewhere of Treve's choosing. He is fond of archaeology and fossils, I am sure he knows where there are lots of such things waiting to be found."

"On their return drive Edith said thoughtfully, "British policemen are very thorough Maree, I do not think investigating teams from other countries would have the patience to go so far for such a little crime."

"Breaking into other people's property is a big crime in England, Edith," Maree told her. "The crime will stay open on the books until it has been solved and the stolen goods found and returned to their owner."

"I wonder how many crimes are solved completely?" Edith mused. "I must ask that nice Constable next time I see him."

When they returned it was time for Maree to report for duty. She made her way to the office in case there were any special messages for her. There was one pinned to the board from Val.

Maree, call from Dawlish. Please ring Barbara. She has urgent news for you!

Chapter 9

"Simon has gone away," Maree's sister told her when she rang her later. "He's walked out of home and office without saying a word even to me. His father seems to think he's taking a holiday on the family motor cruiser somewhere in France."

"But was that planned?" Maree asked.

"Not as far as I know, although he did say it had been suggested he went with you. He also said you were thinking of getting back together. I assumed that meant you were both going with Edith on that trip we talked about when I was with you in Truro."

"Oh, Barbara!" Maree was angry. "How could you possibly think I would agree to him joining Edith and me? I have no feelings except contempt for him. If you hear any more talk like that please nip it in the bud."

"I didn't believe it to be true sis, I'd already started to put a letter together accepting my place at Leeds Uni."

That Maree was pleased to hear. She knew their mum and dad must be delighted at the news, but saying nothing about it to Barbara, she asked, "What happens next?"

"I go for an assessment interview in a couple of weeks. Dad has agreed that he and Mum will come with me. He still has a few days of this year's annual vacation to come, so we are going to make it a bit of a holiday."

"How lovely for you all."

"Truth is, I think they just want to make sure I get into some decent lodgings, but I'm told Yorkshire has some beautiful countryside with lots of green hills and walking areas. I don't want to be cooped up in a little flat in the middle of the city with other students."

"You'll have to take what you can get to start with. You can always change to something more suitable later on."

"Yes, I know, I've already thought of that. Anyway, I really wanted to warn you that Simon will probably show up at Oaklands before long. He's convinced Edith would like him to be with you in France. I think he's talked her into it. He knows about her having property over there, and thinks she has a bit of cash put by. He's persuaded her to become a client on his books. Having said that, he's already broken the rules by talking to me about a client's business, hasn't he?"

"Yes, but I promise not to repeat it. Thanks for the warning. I can't say anything to Edith because she's paying for the trip, so she can invite who she likes to join us, but if Simon does show up I'll try to keep my eyes open. We will have Treve with us. He is very careful of Edith's welfare and already resents Simon's interference, so I don't think he will stray far from her side. Between the two of us we should be able to keep an eye on her."

The next morning, Val asked Maree, "Did you get your message I left last night? I know you often look into the office when you've been out in the afternoon."

"Yes thank you, it was important. Barbara has decided to accept the offered place at Leeds University. Though she really wanted me to know that Mum and Dad would be taking her up for a preview and checking up on digs etc. They might be away for a couple of weeks, so not to worry if I get no reply to letters or phone calls."

"Oh, I'm so pleased for her, how long before you see her again?"

"Probably not until the Christmas break. If she's anything like I was she won't want to come home for short weekends. I roamed the countryside with one or two of the girls who were missing their family and homes."

"Please remember me to her when you speak again. Wish her all the best from me, she's a sensible young lady and deserves to do well."

"Thank you Val, I'm sure she'll be pleased to hear that."

The morning passed without incident. At lunchtime the young policeman dealing with Edith's missing fans rang to enquire if there were any further developments from the Oaklands end. He himself had heard nothing.

Maree assured him he would be the first to know if there was anything to report. She was about to replace the receiver when it struck her she should perhaps warn him of their impending holiday. He requested permission to liaise with Matron while they were away if only to say he would like to speak with her or Edith should they call home.

That afternoon Maree decided not to go to town as usual but to stay and talk to Matron if she was free. They agreed to meet at two thirty. It was as well that they did. It took the full two hours to work out a suitable time for Maree to be away. Val had to be consulted, as she would be required to put in extra hours covering for both Matron and Maree. When she left Matron she agreed to call on Edith the next morning, as she would need to get in touch with Treve.

The last weekend in August seemed the most convenient time for them to leave. Several Oaklands residents would be away, attending a floral festival, Matron said. With hotel accommodation provided for two weeks once they'd gone, this would free Mark to get on with his summer work. There'd be very little porterage to do with so many already away. In between gardening and the small repair jobs he enjoyed, he would be in a better position to check the interior storeroom. Who knows, maybe new evidence regarding the break-in would come to light.

Maree knew where Edith would be at this time of day. As she made her way past the shrubs and flowerbeds in the back garden she thought how lucky they were with the weather, and hoped it wouldn't change too drastically before they went away.

She found Edith in the garden, this time sitting on a bench, a map of France spread out on her lap.

"Oh, I am pleased to see you, Maree." She folded a portion of the map, moving along the bench making room for her. "Have you come to make arrangements for our holiday?"

"Yes, Edith, Matron and I spent a long time yesterday sorting through possible dates. It hasn't been easy and you will need to get in touch with Treve to check that the last weekend in August will be convenient. We must not take advantage of him. He might have other arrangements."

Edith looked at her roguishly. "If you are trying to discover if he has another young lady I must tell you non! He is not a fly of the night."

Maree laughed at the turn of phrase, and gently reprimanded her. "I was not trying to nose into Treve's business."

"I'm sure Treve would not mind you looking into his business." Edith smiled. "I think he would like it if he could look much more into yours."

"I do believe you are trying your hand at matchmaking, Edith, but come in now and we will see that you have everything ready that you wish to take with you."

"But it is another three weeks! Why do we need to pack so early?"

"Maybe I will be busy with other things during the weeks ahead," Maree said. "This is just to make sure you know what to have ready. And supposing the police wish to see us again regarding your fans?"

"Do you think they might find them before we go to France? Should I telephone that nice policeman and ask him to care for them until we return?"

"I suggest you wait until the day before we leave."

Edith seemed happy with the suggestion, and after folding up the map they made their way in to the house. Maree went with Edith to her room, ensuring she put the correct date into her diary.

"Now get in touch with Treve at the first opportunity, Edith, won't you?"

Edith smiled. "Thank you for all your help, Maree. You are good assistant to Matron and to me."

Maree dropped in to the office. Matron was on duty and had hoped Maree would be around. She had some news, but suggested care was taken in what was said to Edith.

"I've had a couple of visitors," said Matron.

"Oh?"

"Yes, Maud and Doreen, the two residents who share Edith's wing."

"Oh dear." Maree was concerned. "I hope they weren't complaining. Edith has been good since we decided on the holiday, and today, because we've chosen a date for leaving, she is particularly happy."

"No." Matron shook her head. Smiling. "No complaints. Apparently in the early hours of the Sunday morning when you and Edith were away at your home, they were in the car park returning from a coach outing and saw a man walking through carrying something about the size of a small suitcase covered in a curtain or a throw."

"Edith's fan cabinet?"

"Possibly. Of course, as it was covered, they didn't know what it could be."

"Did they recognise who it might have been?"

"No, except to say they didn't think he was someone they'd seen working here. What do you think, should we inform the police?"

"Perhaps we should tell Edith first," Maree said, though she hesitated to disagree with her superior. "After all the fans are her property. If we went to the police they would still need to talk to her regarding what procedure to follow. If it really was someone she knows she may not wish to prefer charges against him."

"You could be right. She might be so glad to get her treasures returned she'd not want to take it further."

"I wonder why Maud and Doreen waited until now to talk to you about it?"

"That's easily answered," Matron said. "Apparently they saw the constable here a few days later, that must have been after Mark had informed me of the break in, and surmised that because they weren't questioned there could be nothing wrong, so there was no need for them to do any more about it."

"So what changed their minds?"

"When they returned from a walk yesterday Mark had begun cleaning the interior store, and they asked him if anything had gone missing. He told them he understood Edith had lost some valuables. It was then they realised they might have been witnesses to a real burglary and although they couldn't identify the man, they did wonder if Edith would have given her key to someone while she was away. They talked it over during lunch and finally decided they had better speak to me."

"I think we should talk to Edith. Let her decide how to proceed."

Before picking up the phone Daphne asked, "Do you know where she will be now?"

"I left her in her room."

The phone rang for a short while before being picked up.

"Matron here, Edith, can I call on you before dinner? It is a private matter, but I will bring Maree with me." Matron returned the phone to the rest.

"She will be free in ten minutes."

When Edith let them in she had a suitcase on the bed, and beside it were all the new clothes they had recently bought.

"Thanks for seeing us so quickly, Edith, although time is pressing." Matron proceeded to explain why they were there. "We do feel that the police should be involved promptly. Now that there is a possibility of more evidence they will want to deploy men on the investigation at the earliest opportunity."

Edith took Matron's hand, shaking it. "Thank you very much, Matron, you and Maree are so helpful."

Matron nodded, "Perhaps you will be a little kinder to Mrs Poirot now, Edith. If it wasn't for her and Maud Browning we'd have known nothing of a stranger on the premises that weekend. Whoever it was, he did not call at the office to let me know he was here."

"Oh dear!" Edith shook her head. "There are lots of matters I am not clear about. I wonder how he would obtain a key to the store."

"What about the one attached to your own keys to your room? Could he have got hold of a copy from yours?"

Maree glanced at Edith, who was shaking her head vehemently. She was known to be careful with her keys.

"I do not carry my stores keys outside with me, only my room keys. If I would forget my room keys I wait for Maree. She will let me in."

Maree nodded her head in agreement. The only way someone could have got a copy from Edith's keys was if she had given them hers or they had been taken when she wasn't using them. She wondered if maybe one of the cleaning staff had left the room unlocked whilst she went to do another little task.

"But Matron, my fans would not live in the store room," said Edith. "I would wish to keep them in my own room." She shook her head. "Maybe I make a mistake and do not have them with me at all".

"Well," Matron said. "*We* are not going to solve this mystery, better we hand it over to the police."

Both Edith and Maree nodded in agreement. "So shall we leave it with you, Edith?" Matron asked as they both turned toward the door, "Or do you want me to speak to them?"

"I will talk with them tomorrow" Edith said, "Perhaps I will ring them in the morning and speak with that nice constable. He gave me his number when we talk before." She shook her head as she let them out of her door, adding wistfully, "I did not think I would require it again."

"Poor Edith" Matron said as they made their way back to the office. "I know she is a pest at times but I wouldn't have had this happen to her. If those fans are as valuable as you say, Maree, how could anyone have got rid of them?"

"I don't know," Maree said. "I would imagine the thief would need a pre-arranged deal. In which case they could already have been passed on to a buyer."

Matron returned to her office and Maree went to supervise the staff serving dinner. Later, before returning to her own room, she spoke to, Maud and Doreen, thanking them for their assistance. Coming forward with their observations would be a big help, she assured them.

"If we had only known that man had not got permission to be hanging around the back of the house we would have gone to Matron much sooner than we did," Doreen said.

Maud added, "If I had remembered that you were away we could have followed him, but he must think no one saw him and that he's got away with whatever he stole."

"Please don't blame yourselves," Maree said. "We still don't know what he could have taken from the store. Matron says there was nothing valuable kept in there, only empty cases and trunks."

"We could have been mistaken," Maud said. "He might have been coming from further around the side of the building, he was nearly on us before we saw him. Whatever he carried had either come from inside the house or from the store, it was covered in one of those brocade throws which are usually draped over the big chairs in the lounge. We couldn't even tell what colour car he got into either, because the car park was in darkness and we had just alighted from a brightly lit coach."

"Did you explain all this to Matron?" Maree hadn't heard her mention it to Edith.

"Ooh yes," Doreen said. "She asked us to tell her everything we could remember."

Maree made a mental note to alert Edith for when she spoke again to the police. If he had come from inside the house it could mean he also had a key to someone's rooms. Although if he had come from the back of the house as the ladies suggested, where had he been coming from? Edith's rooms where close to their own.

Maree did not go into the town again that week. She used her afternoons to prepare and pack everything except last minute items. They heard nothing more from the police. Treve arrived on Thursday evening, and after visiting Edith called on Maree to check that everything was in order for them to leave on Friday 21st August.

"The Ferry leaves at 1300 hours and we shall arrive in Roscoff at 1845, a journey of almost six hours allowing for disembarking," he said. "We can have a snack meal if we want on board, but I suggest we get away from the ferry terminal as quickly as possible - I've booked into a hotel for a couple of nights a few miles down the road. We can talk over dinner in the evening and set off early the next morning. I know Aunt Edith will be anxious to reach Montpellier, but I'm not sure if that is the first place we head for."

"Knowing how she likes to exercise, I doubt she will enjoy all the sitting involved." Maree smiled. "She will most likely be glad to stop off somewhere."

"I've no doubt all of us will be more than ready to stretch our legs once we get off the ferry," Treve said. "Of course it does depend how crowded it is. I've done many crossings where it has been easy to get a seat but if it is raining it can be packed with visitors inside. Oh, one other thing, Maree, make sure your passport, and check Aunt Edith's, are to hand before we embark on the ferry please. Now that's all I can think of for the moment. Except to ask, by the way, how has my aunt been these past few days? Have there been any more developments regarding her forgetfulness?"

"No, she has had no bad spells, everything seems to be in order since we arrived at the date for the holiday."

"Good, let's hope that's a positive sign. It has given her something else to think about. Now have you any other queries regarding the holiday."

"No, Edith has filled me in on lots of things. In any case I won't be wandering around on my own, I hope." She looked at him briefly. "As you know I'm likely to run into a language barrier. At the same time I don't want to be a nuisance, so if you and Edith want to go off on your own please tell me. Just point me in the direction of the hotel we're staying in and I'll make my own way and try not to get lost."

He came towards her, taking her in his arms. "You silly girl, I don't want to lose you. If anyone goes astray it will not be you, if I have any say in the matter. This will be an adventure for you too, I hope. I'm looking forward to showing you around. Although I'm not as knowledgeable as my aunt, which she will be sure to point out once we are travelling in her beloved France."

He laughed. "Are you looking forward to it?"

"Oh yes, very much. I'm so grateful to you both. I don't think..."

And there she was prevented from saying any more by a firm

kiss on the lips.

"You talk too much," he said when they came up for air.

Chapter 10

"There is so much to look at, Maree. Are you not happy that you came with us?"

"Yes, Edith, very happy," Maree replied. She had been gazing around her like an excited child, at the same time hoping Treve and Edith had not noticed. There were hundreds of people at the ferry quayside, and so much to see and take in she was totally unprepared for it.

"Though I did not expect it to be like this," she said. "We seem to have been sitting in this queue for an age. Just look at all the coaches. How long does it take to get all the traffic aboard? And what do all the passengers do once they have driven on?"

"Passengers are allowed to get off their transport and make their way up the stairs to the higher decks," Treve told her, pointing to the flight nearby. "When you get up, try not to stray far from your exit. It will be easier to find your way down again."

"There are many interesting things to look at in the duty-free shop," Edith said. "Even if you do not wish to buy at this time you can remember for your return. Ah, now we move."

The parking attendant had begun signalling those nearest the stairs to follow his directions by moving forward and to the right. Treve made it look easy, but not for anything would Maree have wanted to move the car surrounded by so much other traffic, especially the larger, taller vehicles. She breathed a sigh of relief when their turn came and Treve coped successfully. When the people in the car next to them had parked and removed themselves he said it was now safe for them to follow. They managed to stay close together whilst mounting the stairs to the upper decks. On reaching the top Edith whispered something in Maree's ear that she was unable to catch. The next minute Edith had slipped around the folk in front of them and was gone.

Maree turned in desperation to Treve. "Did you see that? Edith has run ahead. I didn't hear what she said."

Treve took her arm. "Don't be alarmed," he said. "This is all familiar ground to her."

Nevertheless Maree wasn't happy until she saw Edith leaning over the rail ahead of them some time later. She took her arm. "Where did you go off to, Edith? You had me worried."

"Ladies." Maree heard the whisper and assumed that was what Edith had said earlier. But Edith did not look her in the eye. Even as she was speaking, she was peering over Maree's shoulder. Then Treve excused himself and she was left holding on to Edith, who, at Treve's leaving, also moved to cross to the opposite rail, where she stood gazing down on to the deck where they had alighted from the car.

Maree decided to see what was interesting Edith. Shock jolted through her. Simon was below, in the act of closing the door of the bright red Jaguar. For the short time since leaving Oaklands and travelling on the ferry she had forgotten his existence. Even the loss of Edith's fans had slipped her mind. Gracious, how awful, the very reason they were aboard the ferry!

By now Edith too had spotted Simon. She waved frantically until he'd seen her. She beckoned him to join them. A short while later he presented himself. Treve too returned, placing his arm over Maree's shoulder proprietorially. If Simon noticed he ignored it; instead he said, "Anyone care for a drink?" Only Edith said yes, which surprised Maree.

"I'll bring her back safely," Simon said, nodding to Treve. "Where will you be, say, in half an hour?"

Treve smiled at Maree. "Now we are under way can I get tea or something for you?"

"Yes please."

"Then we should be somewhere on the next deck down," he told Simon.

Edith looked smart in a navy and white sailor suit styled top and navy pleated skirt, but it was not distinctive enough to pick her out from lots of other passengers, especially from a distance. Maree hoped she wouldn't stray too far, that Simon would take care of her.

Simon shepherded Edith ahead of him. Maree was set to follow but Treve held her back.

"No, we'll wait a moment," he said, "let them get ahead. It's obvious Simon doesn't want to share Edith with us, perhaps he's forgotten that it's possible to buy alcohol and non-alcoholic drinks at the same counter. We could still end up sitting next to each other."

They reached the tea bar in the lounge. After instructing her to take a seat, Treve joined the queue. Maree chose to sit where she could keep an eye on both entrances.

Treve rejoined her with two mugs of tea. "This is OK," he said. "We can see them if they come through here."

"Why do you suppose Simon is also aboard the ferry?" she asked Treve. "Surely he doesn't intend intruding on our holiday?"

"Only he can know why he's here," Treve said. He took her hand. "Look, if he bothers you in any way, tell me. I'll have a word with him."

They spent the next half hour making small talk and people-watching. The lounge was almost filled with passengers. The warm drink finished, Maree excused herself and set off to find the ladies' cloakroom. She was returning when she saw a flash of navy and white ahead of her.

"Edith?" she called. Edith didn't hear her, and Maree hadn't really expected her to. It seemed as though the lounge passengers had more than doubled in the short time she'd been away.

"Maree!" Simon's voice called from behind. She swung round.

"Simon, where is Edith?"

"I think she went to the cloakroom. She spilt something on her skirt and she's gone to wash it off."

Maree was uneasy; she didn't like Edith wandering off on her own. And why hadn't she seen her in the cloakroom? But there were, she realised, several ladies' rooms; she could have been anywhere.

Instead of going through to the lounge, she slipped through a door leading to the outside. Quickly she made her way along to the prow of the boat, where she could again look over to the car deck below.

Sure enough there was Edith, not alone, though Maree did not recognise the distinguished-looking gent she was in earnest conversation with. Dressed in a dark suit, he was holding a Breton-styled cap, which, she imagined, usually covered his thick white hair. Maybe someone connected with the ship's crew, she thought.

Suddenly Edith turned and thrust something into her companion's hand. He swung away in the other direction. Hastily, hoping Edith had not spotted her, Maree returned to the lounge entrance and casually strolled through.

"Maree!" Treve stood up. "We were beginning to wonder where you had got to. Simon said he saw you ten minutes ago, he thought you were headed back here."

"I was," Maree said. "But Simon was not sure where Edith had gone to clean her soiled skirt. I went back to the cloakroom to see if she was still struggling with it. She wasn't there."

"Are you looking for me, or were you hoping I had gone away and not to trouble you any more?" Edith was a shade dishevelled, her face pink with exertion, her humour a little forced.

"So you spilt something on your skirt. Did you manage to get it off, or do you want some help?"

"Oh, yes it all came off with a little rubbing, thank you. The cloakroom ladies have cleaning fluids for everything."

"I think it might be wise to get something to eat before the queue starts to form," Treve said.

"Then I will leave you, I'm not hungry at the moment," said Simon. He stood up and left the lounge.

"Now," said Treve, "let me know what I can get you both. Is it to be hot or cold?"

"I would like to have a sandwich of salad please." If she was staying long enough to eat then maybe Edith was back to normal, Maree decided.

"Same will do for me," Maree said. She hoped Treve might be gone long enough for Edith to tell her who the man with the cap was, but the bar staff were prepared for hungry passengers, and he was back with a well-filled tray before she could do so.

"Simon is going to Provence," Edith informed them.

"Oh?" Treve said, surprised. "Is that where he is staying? Or is he planning on following us around?"

Maree took no part in the conversation. She was annoyed at Simon still attaching himself to Edith, though she would have to agree, if asked, that she could hardly blame him, as Edith was openly encouraging him.

They had barely finished their refreshments when Simon returned in a state of agitation. "Someone has been tampering with the boot of my car," he growled. "I'm sure I left it locked."

"Anything missing?" Treve asked.

"Difficult to tell," Simon said, making himself comfortable on the spare seat next to Treve. "I don't trouble to stow things tidily when I'm on holiday. I tend to do niggling tasks like that at the hotel."

"What about your passport and travel documents? You will be needing those to disembark." Treve didn't try to hide his impatience.

"I have my papers on me," Simon said. "There was an attendant walking up and down between the rows just now, but he was more intent on talking to other people who had remained in their vehicles, or in uniforms like himself, not really paying attention to the cars."

"I hope you have not lost too much good things Simon," Edith said. "I too have lost many precious treasures, though thankfully the good Cornish policemen have a description of the possible thief who take them from my home at Oaklands..." She looked up, as Maree let out a squeal of delight. "But I know how badly you will be feeling."

Simon glanced at her and shook his head. "Don't concern yourself, Edith, they won't get away with it. I will get back what's missing, and then..." nodding his head, "Someone will pay."

As if he'd had enough of their company he stood up, moving away from the table. In his haste to force his way through the crowd he caught his foot on a table leg close by and fell, sprawling heavily into someone carrying a tray of refreshments. The resultant crash as they both hit the deck was shattering, causing concern all round. Passenger attendants were on the spot immediately, but with not so much as a thank you Simon was up and striding out of the exit.

The other man, having been helped to his feet, proved not to be hurt, and left with an attendant to purchase more refreshments. At that moment the man with the Breton cap appeared at the coffee counter. Edith, rising from her seat, darted across the lounge, grasping him by the arm. Chatting amiably for a few minutes, she glanced in Treve's direction. Minutes later they were standing beside the table, an excited Edith smiling at Maree.

He was a handsome man, taller than he appeared when she'd looked down on him from the upper deck, easily six feet and over. His ruddy complexion indicated he had spent many years at sea or working outside in the open air. An upright stance with no unsteadiness, for all he was holding his refreshment tray with both hands, suggested he could have been in the Navy, and well used to the motion of a ship.

She took Maree's hand as he placed the tray on the table. "May I present my great friend, Antoine? Antoine, this is, Maree. She looks after me at Oaklands, the lovely house at Truro in Cornwall where I live. This is my nephew, Treve." Treve had risen to shake hands. "Treve is an archivist and looks after old objects, in - er - a museum," she quickly added as she saw Treve and Maree smile at each other. "And this is Antoine Cluney. We have been friends for many years. Antoine was an English teacher who has now retired."

Antoine smiled at Edith, then turned to Maree. "I also assist with a little police work, for when I finished with teaching I wished to be a private detective. Now in these days it is my greatest pleasure to meet associates of my lovely Edith. As she said, we have a long-standing friendship." He glanced at Treve. "Are you spending some time in France?"

"We are planning on a couple of weeks," Treve told him. "A mixture of business and pleasure." He indicated to Antoine to sit with them.

"But now Antoine is here he will help us to do only a little of the business," Edith hastened to add. "So are you free to join us for dinner, Antoine?"

Maree glanced at Treve, trying to catch his eye. What did Edith mean by her earlier statement, regarding the police knowing about the thief? Now, only a little business? Had Antoine discovered something to do with her fans? Had Edith left them in France after all? She also puzzled what Antoine was doing aboard the ferry. Assuming he lived in France, was it by special arrangement with Edith? She trusted all would be revealed soon.

"Did you manage to have a word with the constable last evening, Edith?" she asked. "You were going to enquire…"

Edith looked at Antoine, a mischievous glint in her eye. "No, I have other people to speak with." Antoine too had a roguish air as he gazed fondly at Edith. In fact the pair of them looked like a couple of rascally schoolchildren.

"I would very much like to join you," he said. "If you would please tell me where you are staying and what time you are to eat."

"We're going on to a hotel," Treve told him. "We are booked in for two nights, mainly to allow the ladies to recover from the journey and indulge their favourite pastime, shop window gazing." Treve pulled the small pad containing the hotel information from his pocket, showing it to Antoine, who smiled and nodded. "Yes, yes, of course I know it, I will direct you. So you've not made arrangements to stay here for several days?" Antoine queried.

"No," Edith said. "The other business may soon be settled, then we can have more holiday. If you have some time to spare perhaps you can come with us. These silly people," indicating Treve and Maree, "think I can remember all the route through France."

"Where is your destination?"

"Ultimately it was to be Strasbourg," Treve replied. "But if Edith's plans change then it will be her choice. We shall probably return to Montpellier after travelling north, then go as fancy takes us. We should be happy for you to join us if you wish and have time to spare."

"I will consult my diary and inform you tonight. If that is convenient to you?" Antoine spoke directly to Treve, but Maree didn't miss the wink directed casually at Edith. She felt even more strongly that prior arrangements had been made.

The journey from the ferry had been well ordered and swiftly carried out. They were now well into France, having chosen to travel through towns and villages, and were planning to take the coast road on their return. Cottages were attractively decorated with pretty floral baskets and window boxes of every size and shape. Cared-for gardens displayed brilliant variations of colour.

Antoine passed them, driving a grey Citroen, and pulled to a stop on the right. Unused to driving on that side of the road, Maree almost cried out a warning as Treve braked, pulling in behind. Antoine climbed out of the car, coming back to them.

"The hotel you are to stay in tonight is thirty minutes' driving from here. Do you wish to look at any place in Montpellier? It is only a short way ahead."

"Edith must be the judge of that," Treve said.

Antoine turned to her. "Well, Edith my dear? Do we stop in Montpellier or no?"

Edith pouted at him. "I do not think so at this time. We will save that pleasure for our return journey."

"What about Simon?" Treve asked Maree, butting in. "Didn't you promise to meet him somewhere?"

"No," she said. "Edith says he was travelling to Aix for en Provence." She turned. "Did Simon say he would meet us somewhere?"

"No, I do not wish to see him. I make no arrangements for tomorrow as we go to Nîmes," Edith said, adding quickly to Antoine, "but only for the meal and a quick sightseeing."

"Ah, land of denim," said Antoine. "I am not surprised you do not wish to stay at Nîmes. At this time of the year the heat is unbearable. But you would, perhaps, wish to see the amphitheatre and other Roman remains. Nîmes is very well served in such buildings."

"What about you, Maree?" Treve asked. "Are you interested in Roman architecture?" Delving into the driver's door pocket and anxious for her not to miss anything, he read from the leaflet he had picked up on the ferry. "According to this the amphitheatre has reopened after its closure for necessary work to be done, and now it can be used for various entertainment purposes, music festivals and theatre revues etc. Maybe you would like it?"

Maree murmured that she would think about it and let him know later. According to Edith there were many interesting places they'd be visiting. She'd planned on making notes separate from her daily journal, with special interest subjects to be topped up from the guidebooks.

"I would like to visit all the theatres," Edith said quietly, "but I can wait for another day. Of course, I have seen them before, but the authorities have been renovating these particular ruins so I have much to learn." She turned to Antoine. "Do they still have the Festival of Opera in July?"

"You are maybe confusing it with Orange, my dear Edith. It still goes on there. If I had known the date of your vacation I would have suggested you came earlier in the year, there would have been time for me to buy tickets for you all." He glanced at his watch. "I think now we should go on to the hotel. I telephoned ahead and I am to join you for dinner, but I think you will perhaps want time for freshening up before you eat."

"We can pick up more programmes at the hotel," Treve suggested. "Then book tickets for somewhere else on our itinerary." Handing his guidebook to Edith, he signalled to Antoine, who was now making his way back to his car, that he was ready to pull away.

"That part of the renovation work which has been done recently we will see on our return," Edith said, as they set off to cover the last few miles to the hotel.

Chapter 11

They were warmly welcomed at the small hotel, where Maree's room was adequately comfortable. Having changed into a blue and white polka dot cotton dress she knocked on Edith's door, and Edith emerged looking pretty in a turquoise skirt and white top.

There were many people already eating in the excellent plush hotel dining room. Dinner was delicious. The menu, written in French and English, saved Maree embarrassment when ordering. They all selected fried chicken, eggs and a selection of spring vegetables with a mixture of salad leaves.

Antoine suggested they stay for the evening entertainment. Between eating and relaxing he filled them in on what they could expect the next day if they wished.

"Montelimar is close by, it is the gateway to Provence, who knows maybe you will see your friend, Simon?" He had not met Simon, so he had the impression that some of them were concerned about him. Treve assured him Simon had no connection with them, or anything to do with their journey. "Montelimar is a busy city, famous for nougat. Provence has its reputation for almonds and honey. If you have a sweet tooth, you will be satisfied and happy.

We can also visit vineyards to buy excellent wine if you would care to do so."

"It sounds delicious." Maree laughed. "But not good for the waistline."

"I think I will have to go much higher in the trees at Oaklands when I go home," Edith said, patting her midriff.

Antoine had been looking through a small black diary. "I have no engagements for the present. My small house in Lyon is being redecorated, so it is in the hands of a caretaker for the next month. I will take much pleasure in joining you on your daily excursions if you wish. I will then return to the mainland, where I have been staying for the last few weeks."

So that is possibly where Edith has been disappearing on those mysterious afternoons, Maree thought.

"That is good," Treve said. "I'm sure we shall benefit from your expert knowledge and enjoy our tour much more."

"If you have no objections, you can travel tomorrow in my car," Antoine said. "In the valley we have good restaurants. They are well known all over France. Many people travel this area just for the food. I know the roads well because I have lived here during my early police duties."

"What do I recall about a large monument erected by a postman?" Treve asked. "Do we go anywhere near it?"

"We can do so, if you wish," Antoine assured him. "It is in the Pastoral hills of the Drôme. The hills rise from the Rhône Valley east of Valence and Montelimar, so you will be very close. It is a wonderful sight. He was self-taught and it took him thirty-three years to build his fantastic masterpiece."

"Oh, you will love it there," Edith interrupted. "The Facteur, and you were right Treve, he was a postman, Cheval, worked very hard to include features from many temples of different beliefs, even some medieval European. He was inspired and determined to complete it."

Maree sat at the table listening to the descriptive chatter. If she never got to see any of the areas they were talking about she felt that she would be able to picture them in her mind. She was so thankful Edith had advised her to bring plenty of scribbling pads, as she called Maree's notebooks.

After their meal the entertainment consisted of two young ladies singing coquettish songs in French, giving a cheeky eye to the men in the dining room. Amidst much laughter they finished their act, curtsied and exited, leaving everyone in a happy frame of mind.

"Will we take a walk before retiring?" Antoine asked. Everyone seemed to be in agreement, so they headed for the door to the outside.

The evening was balmy. Before leaving the restaurant they stood at the entrance to take in what little air there was. Even that was refreshing after the interior warmth, other diners obviously had the same idea for the foyer was crowded. They had barely reached the steps when suddenly someone pushed between them from behind, and Edith went sprawling. The steps were not steep, and had a rail either side for safety. Edith, being petite, fell between the rail and the edge of the steps down into the garden. Treve and Maree rushed down to help her.

Making sure she was not seriously hurt they carried her inside and found a nurse and the manager in attendance. They had been in the office situated off the foyer and had seen everything.

"The clumsy man did not stop," the nurse said. "He ran around the corner and away to the car park."

"That man does not stay here in the hotel," the manager said. "He came only for food. He was travelling alone and arrived in a red Jaguar."

"Please to put the lady down, I will make reparations." The nurse knelt beside Edith as they put her on the large settee. Edith put out her hand to Maree, who grasped it, going down on her knees beside her. While the nurse on her other side bathed the grazes on Edith's knees she whispered, "That was Simon, why would he do such a thing to me?"

Maree confessed she did not know, then asked if she was sure. After all, she was thinking, a red Jaguar was a young man's symbol, anyone could own one.

The nurse placed iodine pads on the wounds, handing Edith a couple of silvered strips containing tablets. "Painkillers, in case you have a disturbed night. You must take two every four hours, but only two. I will give you more in the morning if necessary."

"Will they knock me out?" Edith asked.

"Not unless you indulge in large alcoholic nightcaps, or take all of them in one dose, then I wouldn't want to answer for the consequences." She laughed. "They've never been known to finish off any of my patients. Providing you obey instructions, you will be safe"

"Can I get you a brandy?" Treve asked. But Antoine was already standing by with a goblet in his hand. "I took the liberty of anticipating you, Treve," he said. He handed Edith the brandy, which she placed on the table beside her.

"I think Edith and Maree must stay in the lounge," Antoine said. "Maybe you and I will go for a walk? We will look for the assailant."

"I dare say he is long gone by now," said Treve quietly.

"You will please put that brandy in the lounge for me, Maree," Edith asked as soon as the men had left the room. "I might need to take those tablets later and the nurse said I must not drink alcohol."

Maree did as she was asked, and they spent the next half hour mulling the whole episode over. Maree was still not convinced it had been Simon.

"No sign of him," Treve reported later on their return, "And the red Jaguar has already gone from the car park."

"Edith is convinced it was Simon," Maree said to them. "Though why he should be in such a hurry I cannot think."

"Maybe Edith would prefer to go back to England." Antoine pulled a chair next to where Edith still lay on the settee. "How are your bruises, Edith?"

"I will live." Edith smiled at him. "We will continue with our tour. I have no wish to cut it short and it may be that the worst problem is over now, thanks to you, so we go on. And if I see Simon again I will ask why he has to be in so much hurry."

"I would prefer you leave it to us Aunt, to Antoine and to me," Treve said, smiling down at her. "He would be more careful passing us on the steps."

"Yes, he would not find it so easy to push me over." Antoine flexed his muscles, indicating how strong he could be, and making them all laugh.

"I would like to go to my bed now," said Edith, starting to rise. "Will you help me please Maree?" She slipped the tablets into her purse. Maree noticed there were two strips of four. She hoped Edith wouldn't find it necessary to take any in the night, and if she did that she would be awake enough to realise how many she swallowed.

Having got Edith settled, Maree did not go to her own room but repaired to the lounge and the men. They discussed the incident. If it had indeed been Simon, why would he deliberately hurt Edith? If it had been an accident, why had he not stayed to apologise, to make sure she was not hurt? Treve agreed with Maree. Simon and his aunt were friends, or had been before they had embarked on this tour. On the other hand, if it had not been Simon, but someone else who drove a red Jaguar, then it probably was an accident and they would never see the man again.

Antoine enlightened them as to what had happened earlier on the ferry. Whilst he and Edith were standing talking beside Simon's car Simon had returned to fetch something from the boot.

Antoine had drawn Edith's attention to what could have been the end of her fan cabinet, partially covered by a blanket or curtain underneath a suitcase at the back of the boot.

He had, he said, given his gendarme friends details of the car, together with Edith's snap of its driver, and told the story of Edith's loss. This confirmed Maree's suspicion that Edith had been in touch with Antoine prior to them leaving Oaklands, when they had probably agreed to meet aboard the ferry. The photograph must have been what she had seen handed over.

Word would have been passed around to the various police departments. If seen, Simon would not be apprehended or even spoken to, but Antoine would be kept informed of his movements. He extracted a promise from them not to let Edith know they were aware of it. "All will be revealed in time," he said. Though Edith was almost certain to get her property back, they all agreed it was still necessary to continue to keep a wary eye out for her safety.

Maree called on Edith early the next morning. The nurse was already in attendance. Edith was up and dressed, with the exception of her stockings. The nurse's questions elicited that her grazes were a little sore but she could still walk and had no need of crutches or a wheelchair, but, on the other hand, if they had an attractive, caring young porter with nothing to do for the day she might be able to make use of him for a few hours!

Laughing, the nurse replied that she thought Edith might put the services of a young man to better use if she had no sore spots. She again bathed the grazes, assuring them there was no need for dressings. It would be better to allow them to dry naturally. Maree thanked her, and having helped Edith on with the rest of her garments, both made their way to the dining room.

The men had waited for them before starting breakfast, and very handsome they looked. Antoine had changed the dark suit of the day before for a pale green shirt and beige trousers. Treve was attired in blue trousers and white polo shirt. Edith and Maree wore floral skirts with plain tops. It was a happy foursome that set off after eating.

That day too proved a success, the food at the packed restaurants they visited was as good as Antoine had promised. Although it meant retracing part of their route they returned to the same hotel that night, this time with no untoward incidents.

Next day when they set out again, the hotel manager was there to see them off after wishing them a safe journey with no more problem encounters. There had been no sign of Simon or the red Jaguar.

They broke the journey to spend some hours in Grenoble, an extremely busy city. As well as a thriving industrial centre it boasts a large, outstanding university. No matter where they went the place thronged with young people, but it seemed not only students were attracted to the facilities, even those laid on for the alpine sports. There were also many of an older age group, probably there for sight-seeing, shopping in the fine centres and visiting the museums, especially the fine art which caters for all categories of taste from the ancient to the ultra modern.

They decided to remain in Grenoble for a few days. Antoine and Treve left Edith and Maree in the art department of a museum, instructing them to remain there whilst they went off to find somewhere for them all to stay. The inevitable happened - of course Maree should have been expecting it - Edith disappeared. One minute they were together, discussing the merits of an extremely well executed landscape painting, the next she had gone. On the basis that Edith knew where she had left Maree but Maree had no idea where Edith could be found, Maree felt the best she could do was stay put, letting Edith come to her.

Maree wandered up one side and down the other of the well-stocked gallery. There were beautiful works by artists she'd heard of but never seen, plus several by artists unknown to her. She was deeply engaged in reading the gallery's own catalogue, printed in English, French and German, when the men returned.

"Where is Edith?" Treve asked, "Don't tell me she's left you?"

"Oh hello," she smiled, "I'm afraid she's wandered off alone again."

"Do you know which way she went?" Antoine asked. Maree shook her head. "No, she disappeared whilst I was studying the art on that wall over there, one minute she was speaking to me, the next..." she shrugged.

"Then I will find her." Antoine strode away.

Treve took her arm. "When they return we must go for coffee and something to eat, if that would suit you?"

She smiled up at him. "I should like that, thank you. She sighed. "I do wish Edith would not wander off. I'm not sure what to do, try and find her or stand and wait. At least I had plenty to interest me here."

"You did the right thing, Maree," Treve said. "After all that is what I asked before we left you, If you too had gone from here, Antoine and I would have been hard put to find either of you."

Arms linked, they wandered along to the showcases at the far end of the gallery. Here were lovely miniatures, some in exquisite filigree frames. Details of the authors were clearly written on little cards laid alongside them.

It was here that Antoine discovered them. Treve stared at him, consternation written all over his face. "Have you not found her?"

"Yes, yes, I have found your elusive Edith. She was only in the room next door. Apparently she saw the sign for the relics room. She particularly wanted to see if there were any from the Lyon Mountain area. Now she wishes you to join us for lunch in the restaurant downstairs. Will you please come when you have finished looking around in here?"

"We have finished, we will come with you now."

Treve was a little cool with his aunt, but Maree felt only relief that Antoine had found her. It made her more determined to have a word with Edith, and she planned to do so that evening if the opportunity did not present itself sooner.

Edith was seated near a window at a round table already laid for four. Having no idea how worried Maree had been, she greeted them with enthusiasm.

"Come and sit with me please, we will share lunch together."

Even here in the restaurant, specimens, fossils and relics of ages past were plentiful. Glass cases containing delicate articles including cameos adorned the walls, interspersed here and there with heavily-framed pictures together with a section of ancient maps.

Over the meal, an appetising seafood salad served with brown bread and creamy butter, they talked of the next day's tour in this interesting area, discussing the possibility of visiting neighbouring towns, which also contained museums, universities and colleges of contemporary art. Treve informed them that he and Antoine had succeeded in booking them into a quaint little hotel, which also included a number of separate chalets catering for couples, small families and retired folk.

The first-class meal finished, they strolled around the city, taking in the contemporary art designs displayed everywhere, before wending their way to the car parks and Antoine's car. Treve had already driven his to the hotel they were to stay at.

The hotel was every bit as attractive as Antoine and Treve had promised. Close by were walks of varying degrees of difficulty plus a cable car service. Food in the hotel restaurant was cooked before them on an open brick grill. The weather being fine and warm, the evenings were suitable for al fresco dining.

Sitting on the terrace outside the dining room that evening, Edith excitedly gripped Maree's arm.

"Don't look up now, but the cable car has someone we know on board."

They all stared at her. Maree spoke. "You don't mean Simon? Here?"

"Yes I do, I'm sure it was him, he did not look for us." She started to rise. "Perhaps I can find where the journey ends. I would speak with him."

Antoine took her hand. "No, my friend, we do not go looking for him tonight. I have something special to show you, and that includes you, Maree and Treve, if you would care to join us after the meal is finished."

Edith turned to him excitedly. "Oh Antoine, you are thoughtful, what have you found?"

Well, Maree mused, he had successfully distracted her attention from Simon. Maree too was eager to see what Antoine had to show them, but she had to contain her curiosity for a while as the surprise required Edith and herself to remain in the hotel lounge while the men went off on an errand of their own. They would, they said, be about an hour. An ideal opportunity, Maree decided, to have her long-overdue talk with Edith. In fact it was she who made it easy for Maree.

Taking her arm, she said, "Come with me to my room, I have something for you."

Stopping on the way to tell the manageress, Madame Lefarge, where they could be found if the men returned before them, Maree followed Edith out. Their rooms were on the same floor, similarly positioned on the south side of the building, both overlooking the beautiful valley and the cable car station with its brightly-lit glass windows and gaily-decorated platform. They would have a spectacular view no matter what time of day.

Edith motioned Maree to a chair near the window while she opened a drawer in the pinewood dressing table. Taking from it a package approximately twelve inches square wrapped in brown bubble wrap, she carefully placed it in Maree's lap before seating herself in the chair opposite.

"You may open it," she said. "I hope it will make you happy that you have had such a good holiday. It is also to say I am sorry to make you worry that I go away when you are not looking."

"Oh Edith, thank you." Maree did not immediately open the parcel. Getting up, she placed it on the bed and put her arms around Edith. "I do worry when you go off without telling me where you are going, but that is not all I need to say to you while we have these few minutes on our own."

Edith put on one of her hurt little girl faces. "Have I been so naughty to you, Maree?"

"I do not consider it naughtiness, Edith, I am more inclined to call it thoughtlessness. You rush headlong into actions which if you gave more thought to them you would not do."

Edith looked at her quizzically. "You will explain, Maree?"

Maree released her, settling back in her chair. "Before you get yourself into more serious trouble, you should stop and think. Am I being a nuisance to someone else? For instance, you did not think today and you caused a problem to three people, Antoine and Treve who had to go looking for you, and to me as I was left on my own without being able to speak the language. If someone had come to talk to me, how could I reply?"

Edith leaned forward, taking her hand. "I'm sorry Maree, I promise truly I will not do such a thing again. I will think like you say next time."

"Now," Maree said, "I want to know why you had to shin down the drainpipe at Oaklands when you have only a short walk through the corridor to a door to take you outside?"

She thought for a minute. "It was rehearsal, Maree."

It was Maree's turn to think. Why would anyone need to rehearse shinning down a drainpipe? Oaklands had a perfectly good fire escape. All the residents were given adequate fire drill regularly, and Edith lived on the ground floor.

"But why, Edith? Why would you need to do so? You have no reason to be upstairs."

Edith seemed perplexed that Maree was taking so much interest, and shook her head as she replied. "If one day the players in Truro say I can join the troupe maybe I will have to be a cat thief. I do so once before!"

It took some seconds before Maree realised Edith was referring to cat burglars. "But," she protested, "If you had to play such a part the drainpipe would be built especially safely for actors on stage to use. At Oaklands the pipe could come off the wall and you could be badly hurt."

"So, I must promise not to hurt myself?"

Maree leaned forward, taking both her hands. "I want you to promise not to climb on the pipe again, please? If you need to be upstairs, why not use the lift?"

Edith had been gazing down at the two pairs of hands resting in her lap. Now she looked up. "So if I promise, will you please open your gift?"

In the face of her request, Maree found it difficult to continue. She squeezed Edith's hands, gave her a smile and reached for the packet. The picture it contained delighted her. The scene was of Roscoff harbour; she remembered it being described in her guidebook as the most attractive of the Channel ports. Here was all the hustle and bustle of the ferry unloading. Colourful coaches, lorries and cars were making their way off the ramp and up the slope to the road that would carry them on to their destinations. Brightly-painted inn signs, with old-fashioned names. Private cottages with gay floral decorations much in evidence. She was also reminded that Roscoff was considered the port with the most historical associations with Great Britain.

It wasn't necessary for Edith to ask if Maree was pleased with her picture; the smile said it all. There was no continuing with the gentle lecture she'd intended.

A discreet knock on Edith's door produced one of the hotel's maids with a message to say the gentlemen had returned, and would they please join them in the lounge.

Chapter 12

A gift awaited them. Maree noticed that the men were not forthcoming with information as to their whereabouts earlier, but in the excitement of unwrapping and discovery it was forgotten. Edith's gift revealed a 'Fan Diary'. Issued by a museum in the United Kingdom, it pictured a different hand fan on every page with details of its origins. Tears proved how genuinely touched Edith was.

Maree's own gift turned out to be a view of Lake Annecy as seen from the balcony of a château above it. A booklet accompanied it, which she promised herself she would read later in her room.

"It is where we will probably stay on the next leg of our tour," Treve said as he sat on the chair next to her. Antoine and Edith excused themselves, leaving the room with a smile. "Now how about a walk before we join them?"

"Shouldn't we ask if they'd like to go with us?" Maree asked. "Antoine did say he had something to show us tonight."

"That is to come later. They have gone to ask permission to darken the smaller guest lounge - it is not permitted until after ten o'clock. It is now only nine o'clock. We need not go far, and the scenery is wonderful from many places close by."

"Yes, I'd love to."

Treve squeezed her hand. "Fetch your coat. I'll go and tell them what we're doing and pick you up here in a few minutes."

Happy to know Edith was safe with Antoine, they left by the back entrance. Maree was fascinated with the views, vastly different seen from higher up the hillside and proving the necessity of the chairlifts. Coloured lights emphasised how many other properties were in the vicinity and threw into silhouette the shrubs, hedges and large boulders separating them. Perfume from the garden flowers wafted around them. Maree was sure she could smell old-fashioned Virginia stock, and further on, Nicotiana, one of her father's favourite flowers, reminding her of home.

"This is beautiful, Treve," she whispered. "I never for a moment thought France would be like this."

When his arms came around her she melted into them. As their lips met she returned his kiss.

"Maree, my love." He held her close. "I'm so pleased to have a few minutes alone with you."

Footsteps sounded close by and they broke apart, making their way up the stony track, which, at its end, joined the main road. Here they stopped, allowing the other couple to pass. Once again Maree was overwhelmed with the view below. Treve placed an arm around her.

"If the opportunity ever arises we will come here again, on our own and stay as long as we wish."

"I'd like that," she said. "Edith told me how beautiful France is. I'm not sure I believed her." She added shyly, "But I know the right company can make it extra special". She snuggled closer as his arms closed around her.

Antoine had obtained a video film for their entertainment, hence the blacking-out of the light in the small guest lounge. Fetching the film explained their absence earlier, but not until they were comfortably settled did Maree realise the significance.

The film depicted mainly Lake Geneva and surrounding mountains, and since it had been largely taken from above it was possible to see that the lake really was banana-shaped, as Edith had claimed earlier. Though this was only evident from the air, Maree felt privileged to see it.

Antoine told them later his supplier was an amateur friend who, some years ago, had hired a light aircraft for his filming. He was so pleased with his success that his hobby had now become a full-time profession and it was paying very handsomely. Over late night drinks, however, they decided not to visit Geneva until their return journey. They would instead spend more time at Annecy and its lakeside scenery.

At breakfast next morning Antoine was called to the telephone. When he returned he asked to be excused from joining them for the day's excursion. His attention was required at the local police station. He promised to rejoin them at dinner that evening.

He suggested they would enjoy a visit to Chambery, where they would find other small museums, or, if Treve felt up to driving, they could take the car, pick up one of the brochures containing a map and complete description of the Alpes Gorges, suitable for a day's car touring.

This was said with a suggestive nod toward Edith. Maybe his thinking was there would be less chance of her disappearing in a smaller area or in the confines of a car. Maree did not expect trouble with Edith whilst Treve was with them. She had, after all, promised not to go off on her own without telling them where she was heading. Before leaving the dining room they decided to tour the Gorges.

Treve picked up the brochure to study while Edith and Maree returned to their rooms to change into suitable clothing, flat-heeled shoes and trousers. "In case we have to climb," Edith said.

Maree hoped there would be no necessity for that, but she did as she was bid, returning to the entrance hall to find only Treve had got there before her.

They sat together on a well-cushioned rattan settee, browsing through the brochure and waiting for Edith. Some time later Treve asked Maree to go and see if his aunt was in any kind of difficulty.

It was at that moment that one of the waitresses came through to say that the manageress wished to speak with Maree. Puzzled, she went to the reception desk.

"Madame Arneau telephoned from her room earlier, miss," the woman told her. "She tells me to say to you that she is to join Monsieur Cluney at the police station."

"But we were to meet in the hall, how long ago was that?"

"I cannot tell you miss. I put through a telephone call to her room." She consulted her watch. "Perhaps twenty minutes ago, then I have guests come to make enquiries, and then your friend ring me with this message."

Maree hastily returned to the hall and told Treve what had transpired.

"You stay here," he said. "I will go and check that Madame Lefarge has got it right. Perhaps Edith said something else to her which she has forgotten to mention." But in no time he was back. "No, she claims that was all Edith said, but the lady is puzzled because she knows the police station is not open today."

"But how can that be? Antoine also got a message from there this morning."

Treve was thoughtful. "Perhaps they have skeleton staff on duty, and that is why Antoine's help was needed."

"Then we had better go to the station and make enquiries," she said. "At least we can find out where they can be located."

We will ask the manageress for the whereabouts of the station."

They made their way back to reception, but Madame Lefarge

had nothing more to add. "I told you the local police station is not open today, Monsieur Hocking. If it is urgent you must telephone this number." She passed a small visiting card over to him. "The officer on telephone duty will deal with your enquiry."

"This is getting stranger by the minute," Treve said as they went back to the hall. He peered more closely at the card. "Yes, we'll go there," he decided. "If there is someone answering the phones we might be lucky and speak to them."

As Treve unlocked the car, another car was on its way in. Thankfully it was Antoine's Citroen. Maree was pleased to see him. She clambered out of Treve's car, nearly throwing herself into Antoine's arms.

"Oh Antoine, thank goodness! Is Edith with you?" Though it was clear that she wasn't in his car. Her throat stung, fear now making her shake.

"Edith, no - should she be? Oh, don't tell me she has gone off alone again."

That was it; the tears Maree had managed to suppress spilled over. No way could she control them. Antoine's arms came around her.

"Come, come Maree, you must not let her upset you, it's not the first time, is it? She will return." He shook his head, "I might have known she would do this if I did not go with you."

"It is not quite the same this time," said Treve. He related what had happened after Antoine had left this morning.

"I did not send for her, I can assure you."

Now he was concerned. That someone else was involved in Edith's disappearance was not what he had expected.

"It does answer one other question for me," he said. "There was no official message sent here for me this morning."

"So that is why you have returned early?" Treve said. "We were on our way to the station in the hope of seeing someone who could tell us where we could find you."

"I suggest we go back into the hotel," Antoine said. "We can do nothing without making plans." He glanced at his watch. "It has now turned eleven o'clock. Whoever Edith has gone off with, or whoever has persuaded her to go with them" - he was now voicing all their fears - "has had at least one hour's start on us."

They sat at a window table, and Treve signalled the waitress. "Coffee for three please," he requested. When she returned, Antoine asked if she had seen the taxi driver who had called for Edith.

"Yes monsieur, he wished to know something but I could not help him. I ask the manageress."

Antoine rose. "I will speak with the lady." He followed the waitress out.

Treve took Maree's hand. "Try not to worry, we will find her, and remember what Antoine said, the police are keeping an eye on Simon. He can't move far without being spotted."

"There is good news, I hope," Antoine said as he returned to his chair. "First of all, Madame says the driver was not a genuine taxicab driver. He asked if she would tell him the distance to Lyon from here. She feels he should have known that, as it is barely sixty miles. It would be no more than a local route for him if he was real."

"So, how does that help us?" Treve asked. "Does she think he was trying to put us off the scent by only pretending to be going to Lyon?"

"That is exactly it Treve, she says the man barely raised his head to look her in the eye. He wore his beret more on the lines of a military man, not tilted to the front as most locals do, and she knows of only one man who follows this fashion, a local odd job man known to be involved in all sorts of mischief, though nothing as serious as abduction. And apparently he has never been known to cause harm or injury to anyone."

"Well, I suppose that gives us something to think about," Treve said, "but if Lyon is not his destination, how will we know where he might really be going?"

"This is the good news, possibly. She lives close to a village where the man does a lot of his odd jobbing. Possibly where he picked this one up."

"And what about the car?" Maree butted in anxiously. "Did you mention the colour?"

"I did, she is sure it is green, which is more puzzling. If it was your friend, Simon Markham, the car should be red."

"Oh no," Maree groaned. "He must have changed his car. Now we can't possibly know where he has taken Edith."

"True," Treve said. "We can't just go chasing after all the green cars we happen to see."

"No, of course not, Treve," Antoine said. "But I have a friend in that same village, an ex-police colleague, I will call on him."

Maree stared out of the window. In spite of Antoine's words she feared for Edith's safety. How frightened she must be. And what about food? Edith had a healthy appetite. Would her captor remember to feed her? If it wasn't Simon but some roughneck who just happened to pick on Edith, would he have any compunction about starving an elderly lady? But common sense made her think again. How would a local odd job man know of Edith? Or that she was staying at this hotel?

She shook her head, realising this was getting her nowhere. She dragged her mind back to the conversation between Antoine and Treve.

"So you think our best bet will be to go to this village near Lyon?" Treve was asking.

"Yes, after we have dropped in on my friend," Antoine replied. "We can call at the local police station, and ask if anyone has reported anything suspicious. There are many empty warehouses and other large buildings on the outskirts of Lyon. The local security companies continue to check them out at night. In fact those could be another source of enquiry for us."

"Do you think we should buy some food to take with us?" Maree asked. "Edith could well be hungry when we find her."

"Good idea." Antoine nodded. "Get enough for all of us. We have no idea how long we shall be driving around searching for her."

Antoine went off to refuel the car. It made sense to travel in his vehicle and for him to drive. His knowledge of the roads might help. Recalling that Edith would probably not have had time to collect extra warm clothes, Maree dashed to her own room to fetch a couple of blankets before calling at reception to find out where the nearest food shops were.

Madame Lefarge insisted on a hamper being packed for them. While this was being prepared they were served soup and rolls and told to call her no matter what time they arrived back at the hotel. Her kindness was very much appreciated and when they set off on their desperate search it was with hope in their hearts and her good wishes echoing in their ears.

Maree sat in the back of the car. Treve in the passenger seat at the front could keep his eyes peeled and direct Antoine, should he need it.

With everyone busy with their own thoughts, the first miles were travelled in silence. Maree was certain Edith would not take her abduction, if abduction it turned out to be, lightly. Her mind went back to this morning. Why, she wondered, did Edith not return to the hall to tell them of her change of plan? This also helped dispel the thought that it might have been Simon who had called for her. Barring the incident at the hotel on the first evening - and there was no proof that that was him - one would have thought he'd have wanted them to know Edith was in safe hands.

"Have you heard anything more from your friends regarding the red car, Antoine?" she finally asked, though the lump in her throat was almost choking her.

"The last information which came through a couple of days ago noted that a red Jaguar with an English number plate had been parked for two nights in a car park near Domene, which is not far from Grenoble Airport."

"So he was in the area then?" Treve muttered.

"Simon, or another person driving his car," Antoine said. "I also understand there's been no attempt by him to buy an airline ticket for himself, so we take it that he is still hanging around."

"Then he must be getting about on foot. Or has hired another car," Maree said. "Knowing Simon he won't care for that, he'll be in a hurry to get his problem sorted."

"I don't think it is a problem with the car," Antoine said. "More than likely he now has a liability. A passenger?"

"If he has taken my aunt as an unwilling passenger I can't help feeling he will quickly regret it," said Treve. "She will let him know in no uncertain manner what she thinks of him, and don't forget she is already primed to have words with him."

"I hope she doesn't go too far," Maree said. "Simon is a big man compared with Edith. She would be no match for him if he decided to use strong-arm tactics, and you saw what happened at the hotel last week."

"Do you seriously think he would hurt her?" Treve asked.

"Simon Markham is not above using force to get his own way." She shivered. "Though I must confess to not understanding what he hopes to gain by abducting Edith."

"No doubt we shall soon learn," said Antoine. "Meanwhile we are approaching the outskirts of Lyon. Will you please keep a lookout for a road sign pointing to" - he thought for a moment – "possibly Bourg-en-Bresse, or anywhere with Lyon at the base. We should start to see those directions soon."

"Are there many closed factories around here, Antoine?" Maree asked.

"Unfortunately, yes," Antoine answered. "Lyon used to be the most important centre of the silk industry in France, but not any more."

"But what about the buildings?" Treve asked. "Are they used for other purposes? Perhaps they are rented out."

"The premises are largely used for storing machinery which is still in working order. Security is strict, and they are checked regularly."

"Should we be searching on our own like this, Antoine?" Treve asked. "Maybe the police would rather we called on their help."

"Edith has only been gone for a few hours," Antoine reminded him. "The police would not be happy about arranging a search party for an elderly matron who chooses to go away on her own. If we could prove she has been abducted, it would take only minutes to have a complete force here."

Chapter 13

They were silent for the next mile or so. Traffic was fairly light in this region. When suddenly, without warning, Antoine swung the wheel to the left Maree was taken by surprise and fell over to the other side of the car.

"Sorry, Maree, hold on," he said.

"I'm OK, Antoine," she told him, straightening up. "What happened?"

"Missed the turn-off, sorry, Maree." He reversed, then, taking the correct turning, slowed down in front of a terrace of picturesque cottages.

"Do you want me to get out and investigate?" Treve asked him.

Maree looked out of the window. They appeared to be in a country lane, and judging by the low growing plants in the fields on the other side it could be fruit or grape-growing country. Antoine brought the car to a halt.

"No thank you, Treve, I know this area and some of the people who live here. I will make enquiries. You remain here to look after Maree, we don't want another of our party to go missing." He left them, striding purposefully down the road.

"I'm glad you didn't go off with Antoine," Maree told Treve. "I don't much relish being left here alone under the circumstances."

"I didn't intend you being alone." Treve got out of the car and clambered into the back seat beside her, gathering her into his arms. "I expected Antoine to stay with you, he's done so much already, and after all Edith is my aunt. I thought it right I should offer."

"But he is the policeman," she argued. "He has the authority to ask questions. And another reason, he is a long-time friend of Edith."

"I wouldn't have expected him to have been in this situation with her though," Treve said.

"Maybe not with Edith, but no doubt he has had experience of other abductions."

"I've told you before, you talk too much," Treve whispered as he hugged her to him.

Maree sat, blissfully content to be in his arms. This was how a holiday should be, she decided, if only there were no... but how could she wish there were no other people? She wouldn't be there herself if it weren't for others.

She struggled to sit up. "I wonder how Antoine is getting on. Has he discovered anything?"

"You can ask him yourself, he's approaching now."

And there he was, striding up the lane alone. She hadn't really expected him to return with Edith, but she'd half hoped.

"Anything of help, Antoine?" she asked as Treve clambered back into the front seat.

"Nothing at the present time I'm afraid," he said. "But there's something to investigate later in the day, and before I say any more, I need a coffee. Edith-hunting is thirsty work."

"There are two flasks in the hamper, if there is time of course, but" - she glanced at Antoine - "perhaps we..."

"Good, we'll all have lunch," Antoine said. "If that is all right with you, Treve? It is quiet here, and we're not causing an obstruction."

Treve got out, going round to the boot. Before returning to his own seat he passed the hamper in to Maree. As she removed the flasks and poured the coffee, Antoine told them of his enquiries.

" Further along on the left is a disused barn and the remains of an old farmhouse once lived in by a family who moved away to another area. The empty property has been sold, but so far the new owners have not moved into it. It was a remark by my friend Madeline about it still being unoccupied that sparked off the conversation."

"I don't suppose they've seen anything suspicious in the empty house?" Maree asked, handing over the hot drinks.

"Not at that particular property," Antoine replied, "but some metres down the lane is a disused monastery. Alice and her husband, who happen to be visiting Madeline today, are the owners of the gîte opposite that particular building, and recently they have had an English couple call on them asking for details of the owners. They also claim to have seen a light flickering about the old building a few evenings ago. He has been toying with the idea of going over in daylight and if he found anything that made him suspicious, such as locks damaged or windows interfered with, he was going to ring the police station."

"Why hasn't he done that already?" Treve was puzzled. "Did he think he might be caught trespassing?"

"No," Antoine smiled. "They are of retired age. It was simply that his wife was not happy for him to do it on his own in case he fell and hurt himself, so I have persuaded him to let me accompany him. I'm sure two pairs of eyes will be of greater use and together we will be more than capable of dealing with problems, if there are any."

"So, when are you going?" Maree asked anxiously.

"Later on - they plan on leaving here around five o clock. All four friends are occupied with business matters until then. I could hardly ask them to leave any earlier on an offchance that someone might be using the premises illegally, could I? And they do have to obtain the key from the holder, who is also a working businessman and only available after five o'clock."

Having complied with a request for more coffee and a baguette, Maree waited a short while before asking him a question that had crossed her mind many times since meeting him.

"How did you and Edith meet, Antoine?"

For some minutes he remained deep in thought. She wondered if she had been indiscreet, but then a smile appeared on his face.

"As a young man I moved from England with my parents to Lyon. They owned a château, which they ran as a hotel. I attended a local academy where I studied history and criminology. This afforded me a lot of spare time. I joined the local police cadet force, and would you believe I became a stage door johnny?"

"That's someone who tries to get stage artistes to see them after the show has finished, isn't it?" Maree asked.

"Yes, I was interested, in the nicest possible way of course. Edith was appearing at a variety theatre in an all singing, all dancing performance. The show's reputation was such that the police had to provide extra guards at all exits and entrances to protect the artistes. As senior cadets we were in our late twenties and every one of us fell in love with Edith."

"I'm interested in this period of her life," Treve said. "I've never liked to ask her about those days. It was an unhappy time for her around then."

"Of course, none of us realised she was married. Most of my colleagues were already spoken for. I was a bachelor with no attachments, and enough money to go to the theatre frequently."

"Lucky you Antoine," Maree smiled, imagining these earnest young men chasing after the female singers and dancers.

" One night," Antoine continued, "being alone, I decided to wait around after the show and speak to her when she left."

" Trying to gain an advantage over your friends," Maree suggested.

"That was what I had hoped," Antoine agreed. "I didn't hang around the stage door but waited a little distance off. At last two of the girls emerged together, and one of them was Edith. As they stepped on to the pavement a car pulled up. Two young men got out and lunged for the girls. They managed to grab one of them, but weren't able to force her into the car. The other was Edith, and she set about them with handbag and fists. They had to release the girl they were holding. Before they could grab either of the girls again I and a passing gent, seeing the incident, had got hold of the young men and forced them back into their own car. The driver didn't hang around."

"Well done Antoine," Maree said. "A shame there wasn't someone to help her today."

"I dare say my aunt went willingly today," Treve said. "After all, she thought she was meeting Antoine and maybe going somewhere special with him."

"It is a pity Edith can't remember the code we used when we were friends all that time ago," said Antoine. "She would have known that the message delivered this morning hadn't come from me."

"A code?" Maree said. "That sounds interesting! I must ask her about it next time we are at a loose end. Unless she has forgotten it."

"Why would a code be necessary between you?" Treve asked.

Antoine shook his head before replying. "Edith and I remained friends after she told me she was married, and her husband, Luc, also became a friend. After Luc's accident she was no longer able to act on the stage because of caring for him, so she took on the job of dressmaker and repairer to the other artistes. Luc was confined to a bed-chair by this time, so while he slept in the afternoons she sewed. It brought her in a few francs which helped pay the bills."

"But a special code, Antoine? Surely you could call to see them?" Maree was truly puzzled.

"Edith often shopped in the mornings. The nurse who came into bath Luc and change his dressings was protective in a most possessive way. I think she may have been friendly with Luc's family and could have been told he wasn't to be visited except on the days his mother was in attendance."

"But why?" Maree queried. "Surely the family would have been only too pleased for Luc to have friends prepared to visit him."

"We assumed it was so that she could vet his callers. I got into the habit of dropping into the theatre and leaving notes for Edith with the doorman to arrange my visits for afternoons only. Once a note was left asking me not to call at the house again, as theatre folk were not considered suitable company for a sick man and I was known to be a frequent visitor to the theatre."

"That was a bit stiff, Antoine," Treve said. "What did you do?"

"I took a chance and called on a day when I knew Edith didn't shop. We decided that someone was intercepting my notes. We had to put a stop to that. Luc always seemed bright enough when I was there to talk to him. So the three of us devised the code."

"May we ask what the code was?"

"There's no harm in you knowing now, it might come in useful between you and Edith one of these days. It was to mention a garment, a white cardigan."

"Why specifically a white cardigan, Antoine?" Maree was intrigued by the revealing of this secret of Edith's.

"There was an occasion when the dancers in one of the shows were all dressed completely in white and one girl turned up at full dress rehearsal in a red top. The director was furious. He sent her away and insisted she did not return until she had found her elusive white. Edith was relating this tale the day before the dismissive note arrived for me. When we needed a suitable code she immediately suggested white was for peace, and to allay suspicion what could be more natural for a seamstress than to refer to a garment? So the code words became 'white cardigan'. If we received a note with no reference to a white cardigan we knew it could not be genuine, that it had not come from either of us."

"I can imagine her getting some quiet satisfaction from outwitting who ever had sent that uncharitable message to you, Antoine," Maree said.

"It worked though. We had no more trouble." He handed her his empty cup and rolled-up serviette. Treve also passed his over. "That was satisfactory. It will keep me going for a few more hours," he said.

Antoine glanced at his watch. "We have a couple of hours before I need call on our friends," he said.

"You also have to call on your policeman friend, Antoine," said Maree.

"Yes Maree, but we can combine the two, I'm sure."

"What a good idea." Treve turned around. "I'm sure Maree must be in need of stretching her legs?"

How right he was, Maree thought. She seemed to have been cooped up in Antoine's Citroen for days, though in truth - she glanced at her watch - it was only four hours. She repacked the hamper and Treve got out to stow it away. It was only then that she realised that since they'd arrived in the lane she had not seen another vehicle of any description.

"I take it this lane is not much used?" she asked Antoine.

"The lack of traffic, you mean?" Antoine swivelled round in his seat, as Treve arrived back in the car. "At harvest time, you would not find a spare car space anywhere. The friends I've recently visited have often to call out the local traffic police to remove illegally parked cars from *inside* their driveway. Next day there are others parked in the same place. The residents refuse to have lines painted outside their property, claiming they are unsightly."

"Surely a notice could be strategically placed?" Treve remarked.

"You would think so wouldn't you?" Antoine said, fumbling in the door pocket. "It has been tried, but they are always destroyed, and no one can be sure who the culprits are."

"Then they have to put up with the inconvenience," Maree said.

"I'm afraid you're right, Maree. Now give me a minute to look at the map. Ah! as I thought, we are not far from Fourvière. It will take only a short while to drive there. I will call at the police station as maybe another of my friends will be on duty there, and I can enquire if he has any information."

"What if your friends remember something more about those mysterious lights in the building down the road?" Treve asked. "Shouldn't we be on hand in case they want us?"

"If you had seen the paperwork concerning the business they still had to deal with after I left them I doubt if they will have time to think about anything other than that, before I return."

After calling at the home of his local policeman friend and learning nothing new, Antoine drove on into the town, where they decided to visit the Museum of Historical Tissues, agreeing that once they'd made use of the cloakrooms, they'd decide what the next move should be. After all, there was still some time before their expected return to Antoine's friends. Marie was anxious not to waste that time. So when Antoine suggested that he should visit the local police station, as there was always a possibility that someone had reported a disturbance at a disused factory site nearby, Maree and Treve reluctantly agreed to remain where they were, on condition that he wouldn't be away long.

Maree had expected the museum to be filled with Lyon silk, but interestingly this was not so. There was silk, from many countries, also satin, damask, cottons and some fabulous lace garments with accessories. Not far from where they stood there were stage costumes reminding her of the postcards Edith had shown her some weeks before at Oaklands.

She sighed. "You know, Treve, if Edith had a choice as to where she'd be taken this would be the place. She would love it in here."

"I tend to agree, Maree" he said, taking her hand. "Needlework and stage costumes all under one roof - this would be no hardship for her."

Unfortunately the identifying tags were written in French and though Treve was happy to translate them for her, Maree couldn't really concentrate on what he read.

"It is all lovely." Sadly she shook her head, "If only Edith were with us. Oh, Treve what are we going to do about finding her? Antoine doesn't seem too anxious, almost as though he expects her to turn up shortly."

"You must realise, Maree, he does know her better than either of us. I do feel though, that he is concerned this time. Let's hope they find her quickly or soon establish that there is no one in those premises, or it might become necessary to look for somewhere to stay the night." He glanced along the aisle. "Ah, here's Antoine. Any news?"

"No, nothing of any help to us I'm afraid. Now I think we must hurry back to our picnic spot."

As Antoine drove, he reminded them of what he and his friend would be doing.

" I hope you won't be taking too many risks," Maree said.

"Only a small risk, but if anybody sees us enter the building and objects, we will explain why. If the property belongs to them they will want to help I'm certain, so you must not concern yourself, Maree. We should be safe, and if our dear Edith is there we will find her."

Antoine parked the car some way past the cottage Madeline's friend lived in. He advised that if anyone were to question them

131

they had simply to say they were English. He withdrew a map from the door pocket, handing it to Treve.

"Keep this open on your lap, it will convince them you are trying to find your way," he said. With that he shut the door and turned back the way they had come, to disappear through the gate of his friend's cottage. Treve slid across to the driver's seat, and Maree moved on to the front passenger's seat.

Then another vehicle arrived in the road; a motorcycle. When it pulled in some way behind them they bent their heads over the map in case the driver should be heading their way, which he did. He tapped on the window. Treve wound the window down half way.

"Can I be of assistance?" The voice was English. Maree looked up to see a young man, possibly in his late twenties, gazing in at them.

Treve carefully folded the map and wound the window down fully. "That's very kind of you, but no thank you, we're not in difficulties," he said. "We are waiting for a friend who is calling at a cottage nearby." He indicated behind the car.

"Oh, are you friends of Antoine?" the man asked, removing his helmet.

"That's right," Treve smiled. "Then you know him?"

"We met briefly at my aunt's. I'm Phillip Wells, staying here for the summer hols." He offered his hand through the open window but Treve, passing the map to Maree, opened the door and got out. Phillip straightened up and shook hands. He was a fit, athletic young man, Maree decided, taking in the sportsmanlike figure. She felt sure he could be useful in helping Antoine search for Edith.

"Why didn't you go with Antoine? My aunt would have made you welcome," said Phillip. He walked around the car, smiling, to shake hands with Maree.

She smiled back. "That would have been an imposition.

Besides, we are seeking the whereabouts of Treve's aunt. We don't want to waste anyone else's time."

"Ah, yes, the lady who has disappeared. Well that is why I have returned. I will go with my uncle and his friend to the old building. I used to wander all over it with my chums in the school holidays. I remember some of the hiding places. Maybe I can help."

"Do you think there might be a chance of someone being hidden in there?" Treve asked.

"I would not like to imagine anyone shut in there for long," Phillip said. "It has been unused for some time. There is no fresh water nearby and unless food was brought in on a regular basis I would not think it could possibly do any good for one's health."

"Then we must hope she is not being held in there, or any place like it," Treve said.

Phillip strolled back around the front of the car. "I wasn't present when Antoine told my aunt the full story. How long has the lady been missing?"

"A few hours only," Treve replied. "She went away in a green car after breakfast this morning. Our problem is we didn't see her go, we've no idea what she is wearing, and we didn't see the driver of the car who collected her."

The young man looked thoughtful. "Then if you are sure you will not come to my aunt's, I will leave you for the present. No doubt we shall meet again later. I would like to know how the search goes."

"Thank you for offering, we are very grateful," Maree said.

"Yes," Treve echoed. "If my aunt is found soon you may be sure we will see you are informed."

"He appears to be a fit young man," Maree said to Treve as Phillip made his way to the cottage gate Antoine had previously entered. "If he really knows that building as well as he claims, he could help Antoine a lot."

"He can certainly save some time," Treve agreed.

Maree felt a degree of optimism whilst chatting with Phillip, but once he had left, the worry over Edith returned. There was no obvious reason for her abduction, and she could think of no one who would wish her harm. If her husband's family was involved, what did they hope to gain? Surely they had no interest in her future, having already benefited by Luc's death? There were no children, and it seemed there was no way Edith could be making a claim on her late husband's estate. The only possessions left were Edith's own, such as the boat, and those, according to Treve, were to be sold.

Chapter 14

"Ah, here comes Antoine, with company, I'm pleased to see," said Treve, interrupting Maree's sombre thoughts. In a few minutes Antoine did appear, together with Phillip and another gentleman and a woman, who were introduced as Henry and his wife Alice.

"Alice has come to take you to the cottage, Maree," Antoine said, opening the car door. "Treve can come with us. Henry tells me there are so many small rooms in the building that the more there are of us to search the better."

"That is very kind, are you sure we are not putting you to any trouble?" Maree asked.

"My dear," Alice smiled at her, "Of course you are no trouble. Besides, like you good people Henry and I are English. I shall be only too pleased to have a talk with a fellow countrywoman."

Maree got out of the car and waited while Antoine locked it.

"We will be as quick as we can be," Antoine said. "With four of us to cover the building it will be much easier."

"Please be careful," Alice said. "I will have tea prepared for your return."

"Yes, do take care," Maree added.

Alice took Maree's arm as the men walked away. "Come, Maree, we will go and have a cup of tea."

Maree looked at Alice; she had not expected such an English response.

"Did that surprise you my dear? Well don't be, even here in France the cuppa is still the cure all for us Brits."

Maree laughed. "I'm sorry, was I that obvious? I'd always imagined that only coffee was drunk in France."

"Then you haven't been to France often?"

"No, this is my first visit."

They had reached the cottage. "Such a pretty garden," Maree exclaimed. "Is this your handiwork?"

"I plan it, Henry grows the plants from seeds and cuttings and we plant them together. We are both retired from our office jobs, so the garden is a full-time hobby for both of us. That and a couple of days shopping monthly at the market is our life now."

Alice unlocked the door and ushered her surprise guest in to a remarkably pretty room. Ecru coloured lacework was everywhere, on cushion covers, chair-backs, table centres and curtains. All made of lace.

"Make yourself comfortable, Maree, I'll be with you in a moment."

Maree looked around. An Ercol-style suite had pride of place. The rich autumnal colours of the tapestry, set against the darkly varnished woodwork, was warm and inviting. In front of the window was a high-backed bench. With plump cushions covered in lace, this too begged to be sat on. She did so. Set against the far wall was a dining table. A folded tablecloth and a small wicker basket filled with cutlery rested on it. Hanging randomly around the walls were embroidered pictures, mainly of animals. In the recesses, shelves held sparkling glass ornaments. On the floor, rugs covered slate slabs. The whole gave off a pleasant sense of peace and comfort.

Alice came in carrying a tray. "Ah good, you've seated yourself, are you comfortable?"

"Oh yes, thank you! What a lovely room. Did you work this beautiful lace?"

"Not all of it, Maree. Some was done by my mother when she was still with us. Unfortunately since taking up gardening full time my hands are no longer in a fit state. Now what will you have? Tea, coffee or...?"

"Tea please."

"This is so kind of you," Maree said, when Alice returned with the steaming cup.

"It's got to be better than sitting in a car alone while the men are gone." Her hostess smiled.

"Yes, it is and I am grateful to you." She didn't mention that Treve had not intended going with Antoine, so he would have been with her in the car. What were they doing now? She felt the need to talk, anything to take her mind off the men and the search.

"This appears to be quite a fertile area. What is it I noticed growing in the fields, Alice? Vines?"

"No, it is soft fruit. Several of the farmers here have diversified from wine grapes to fruit for the markets. With the growing numbers of folk from outside France coming to live in the country there is an increased demand for market produce. All good for the economy of course."

"Cheese and apples from France are two products Edith often has me looking for in our stores at home," Maree said.

"How long since your friend left France?"

"Two years or more, I believe."

"Then she will notice many changes in this district," Alice said wistfully.

"The loss of the silk industry must have caused a lot of hardship," Maree suggested. "There are quite a number of closed factories, aren't there?"

"Oh yes, and most of the folk who lost those jobs have now left the area for good. This is one of the reasons so many properties are up for sale."

"You have lots of visitors. The ferry was crowded on the day we came across."

"Yes, we do. Tourism is a good money-spinner of course, in fact it is often reported that we have more visitors holidaying in this country than home-staying natives. Lots of them spend their time going around looking at properties for sale, and it is the summer and autumn when the private houses get snapped up."

But Maree could not forget why they were sitting in this stranger's house making idle chitchat. The men had been gone for ages, it seemed. She was aware of Alice's eyes on her, and controlled the urge to look at her watch.

"You are getting anxious, aren't you?" said Alice. "Don't be. If she is anywhere in that building they will find her. Phillip has been holidaying with us ever since he first started school. Once the monastery closed we couldn't keep the boys out of it. He must know every nook and cranny."

Maree swallowed dryly. "But I can't help feeling that if she's not there, we are wasting time."

"Which could be better spent looking elsewhere, you feel?" Alice came over to sit beside her. "Think about it, Maree, they had to start somewhere, and there has to be a reason for those lights we saw in a building which has not been used officially for many years. The security firms also stopped checking the premises a year ago."

"Then that means it has to be someone who knows the area, who knows security is slack and they are not likely to be caught in the premises."

"You are probably right." She glanced at her watch, "I must switch the oven on, the men will be hungry when they return. Come with me. You can look over the kitchen garden and see what we do when we are not indulging our taste for pretty flowers."

Maree followed her into a large kitchen. Herbs, bunches of onions and even small hams hung from beams, which like the ceiling were painted cream. Here too, hand-worked lace was in evidence. The scent of lavender indicated its presence amongst the herbs. Alice flicked a switch on the wall.

"What a lovely room," Maree exclaimed. "It must be a pleasure working here."

"I like cooking." Alice smiled. "And I enjoy spending time in the kitchen. We have quite a variety of wildlife visit the garden too, which I feed regularly, so even when the chores are finished there is a lot to keep me interested in here."

She indicated a small doorway to the outside. This garden was orderly. with plants laid out in neat rows. Maree was able to recognise most of them, having seen them in her father's garden at home. She followed down the central path as Alice pointed out the varieties of green vegetables. Some Maree had not heard of, but Alice assured her it wouldn't be too long before they appeared in English markets.

As they reached the end of the path Maree realised it was now dusk, and the little plants were becoming difficult to pick out.

"It all looks very efficient, Alice, do you plant the same every year?"

"Mostly we stick to the same varieties, those we like to eat ourselves. The few friends and neighbours we supply are also keen on them so it makes sense not to change too often." Excitedly she grabbed Maree's hand. "Here are the men," she exclaimed, hurrying Maree along the path.

Maree needed to watch where she was putting her feet. She heard the voices but they were too indistinct to recognise. Then she was in the kitchen. The front door opened as she stepped into the pretty sitting room. And there was Edith.

Maree dashed forward, taking her in her arms. "Edith! Oh,

Edith!" She hugged her tightly. "Oh it's good to see you. Are you all right?"

Squirming, Edith extricated herself. "Please do not make so much demonstration." Maree stepped back, realising she had embarrassed her friend.

"Of course I am well," said Edith.

"Please take a seat." Alice hovered as the men edged past. "You can talk over your meal." She was pulling out the table as Henry stepped forward to take the men out through the door leading to the kitchen.

"But we can't impose on you any longer, Alice," Maree said. "You have been so kind. We owe you a great debt already."

Keeping her back to them while she placed the cloth on the table, Alice replied, "Then you will repay me by staying for the food which is already prepared. And you cannot leave until we have assured ourselves that your friend is in no more danger. Or if she needs a doctor?" She turned. "You are forgetting your manners, miss, you have not introduced me, nor have you asked her if she has eaten."

"Oh, I am so sorry."

She drew Edith forward, making the introduction. Alice kissed Edith on both cheeks. "Come with me," she said, leading her to the foot of the stairs. "Up there the first on the right is the bathroom, you must feel the need of it after a day in that dreadful old building. When you come down I will have a hot drink ready". Coming back into the room, she smiled at Maree, "Your friend will feel better soon" she said, carrying on through to the kitchen.

Later she returned with a tray holding four mugs of coffee, placing them on the table for the men. Edith returned and Alice led her to the settee.

"Sit there dear, now what's it to be, tea or coffee?"

"Coffee please." Edith's voice was still quiet.

Maree stood, touching Alice on the arm. "Can I help?"

"No thank you Maree, stay and keep Edith company. I'm sure she has spent enough time on her own today."

Sitting on the matching chair across from Edith, Maree watched her as one by one the men returned to the room, selecting a cup of coffee before sitting and nodding at Edith to assure themselves she was OK. She was surprisingly tidy for someone who'd had no access to a washroom or mirror for the day. Maree noticed a few snags in her brown trousers, and threads pulled in the fawn woollen jumper. The silver hair, which she was particularly fussy about on normal days, was flattened on one side. No doubt she'd be more than happy to return to the hotel and make use of its adequate bathroom.

Treve crossed to sit beside his aunt, placing one arm across the back of the settee. "So, how does it feel to be back in the bosom of your family?"

"It feels good, but I am tired," Edith responded with a slight nod of her head. "I thought I would be there for the whole of the night."

Antoine placed another chair on the other side of her and sat, taking her hand.

"There was no chance of that happening while I was still able to walk, Edith. You might have known Treve and I would not let you escape so easily."

"But how did you find me? The man who came to fetch me with the green car this morning said only one English man was interested in where I was. He said he had to keep me safe until that man was ready to come to take me to a boat."

"Did he mention the man's name?" Maree was still convinced it was Simon.

Antoine shook his head. "I have already asked. Edith did not recognise him from her captor's description. Perhaps it was the assailant who knocked Edith down the steps that night."

Alice came in with a cup of coffee for Edith. "You will drink it, won't you? Don't let these men talk you out of it. Their questions can wait."

Yes, Maree thought, Edith is safe now. The questions can come later. She too rose, following Alice into the kitchen, intending to speak with her. Phillip came in from the garden.

"Maree, she is OK is she?"

She guessed he meant Edith. "Yes, a little subdued but that is to be expected. When she realises she is safe amongst friends again no doubt she will relax."

"I don't think she was in any danger," Phillip said. "From the conversation she had with the car driver he was instructed to stay close to her but had no liking for the job."

"So, she was alone when you found her then?" Alice asked.

"Yes. He had left her some time earlier, locking her in an upstairs room, but later in the day he'd pushed the key under the door. Apparently his orders were that once he'd made sure she was secure he was to lock the doors and take the keys with him when he left."

"He didn't intend her any harm then?"

"No, the plan was she should remain in captivity until someone else collected her. He told her he would leave her the key, but she was to decide for herself how to get out of the building. He would figure out how to get the key back from her another day. That way it wouldn't look as if he'd had anything to do with her escape."

"So how did you find her?" Maree asked.

"She wasn't in the building at all," Phillip smiled. "I don't know how she'd managed it, but somehow she had got out and had moved into an outside building."

No, Maree thought, you do not know our Edith. We who do could tell you it wouldn't take her long to figure out an escape route.

"We found her curled up on a shelf," Phillip continued. "In what had once been a laundry drying room. It was dry and contained tables and shelving. There were also lots of cloths. They were a bit smelly but nothing more than that, so if she had needed to use them as bedding it wouldn't have been too bad."

"That won't be necessary, thanks to you and your friends. We can't thank you enough."

"It's really thanks to Antoine," Alice said as she took Maree's arm. "If he hadn't called in to see Madeline today Henry would never have plucked up the courage to go into that building. Now, come," she said brightly, "We will see if everyone is ready for a meal."

"This is very good of you." Maree squeezed her hand. "We did not expect you to go to so much trouble."

"It is no trouble, I am more than pleased to help, and just think what you have given us! Such an adventurous day! What a story we have to tell friends who come to visit. I trust you will not return to England without calling on us before you leave?"

Antoine, standing by the table with Henry, overheard Alice's words, and hastened to reassure her as they entered the room.

"Of course not Alice, we will call on you. I have also promised to visit Madeline. After the assistance you've all given today we wouldn't dream of leaving France without seeing you again. Edith too will want to thank you herself, once she has recovered from the ordeal."

While she had been absent from the room, someone, Maree assumed it had been Henry, had set the table with the serviettes and cutlery. Edith still appeared quiet and subdued, though she moved willingly enough at Alice's call.

"Please sit at the table everyone."

It occurred to Maree that Edith might not have eaten since breakfast. She glanced at her watch. It was well past eight o'clock.

After assuring herself they were all settled at the table Alice left them, to return minutes later with Phillip. Both were carrying trays. Two steaming pies plus dishes of vegetables – no doubt from the garden - were placed on the table, followed by a dish of creamed mashed potatoes and a large bowl of green salad, all accompanied by a platter of assorted cold meats.

They helped themselves and tucked in heartily. Glancing around the table Maree wondered how often Alice had seven people to cater for. She hoped Alice realised by the fact that they had cleared their plates how much her efforts were appreciated.

The food was delicious. Maree had very little room for the fruit salad and cream that followed in spite of taking only a small helping. Like the men, she chose to drink her coffee standing. She tried to talk to Edith, but though she answered readily enough when spoken to she was not as forthcoming as she could be. Treve also seemed puzzled. In view of what she'd been through perhaps they should not have been surprised, Maree told herself. Possibly she was reticent because of being in a room with strangers. Maybe once they were in the car on the way back to the Grenoble Hotel she might come out of her shell.

It was late by the time they reached the hotel. Antoine had telephoned ahead, so Madame Lefarge was ready for them. She had small pastries, biscuits and hot drinks waiting. She made a great fuss of Edith, hoping she had not come to any harm at the hands of the man in the green car. Edith assured her that he had been a gentleman, that she had not been hurt in any way.

When Edith decided it was time for bed, Maree offered to accompany her to her room. Edith seemed to welcome the idea. She came from the bathroom already in her nightwear. In her bed she indicated Maree sit on it. Keeping her head lowered, she took Maree's hand, and in a tearful voice begged to be forgiven.

"For what?" Maree asked.

"I did not keep two promises to you," she whispered.

"But you hadn't much choice in…"

Edith put two fingers over Maree's lips. "Hush," she said. "You must listen to me please."

Gently Maree pushed the fingers away. "You have no need to explain, what happened wasn't your fault."

"First," Edith continued as if Maree hadn't spoken, "I go away without telling you where I was going, and then to add to my crime I break my other promise to you."

Maree shrugged. Whatever? It was obviously troubling Edith. Maree let her continue.

"He pushed the key under my door, voilà! I can get out! But the big door down the stairs was locked with a different key so I have to go up to the room again to think what to do next. Then I search inside all of the building for a long time. I find the only way out of it was through the window on the top floor. So I think there will be a fire escape, non, that too I cannot find."

Maree should have guessed what was coming. She had to lean close to hear what Edith was saying.

"I slide down the drainpipe. But I did not hurt myself," she added quickly.

Maree gathered Edith to her, and this time Edith did not flinch or pull away.

"Oh, Edith! You must not upset yourself. You had no choice. Suppose you had stayed until the other man came for you? We would never have found you."

Edith gazed up at Maree with tear-filled eyes. "Then you are not angry with me for breaking my promises?"

"Of course not, it was special circumstances. Now lie down and try to sleep. We can talk again tomorrow."

Edith squeezed Maree's hand. "Were the men angry with me, Maree?"

"No, they were very concerned you might be lying hurt somewhere."

"I would have walked away from that place if the men had not come for me. I think to myself I must wait until it gets dark before I leave, then nobody would see me."

Maree tucked the bedding around her. Edith breathed a deep sigh, obviously relieved she hadn't got herself into any more trouble. Maree realised too why she had been so tense earlier.

Maree found sleep didn't come easily to her in spite of the long day travelling and the relief at its end. Over and over she struggled to find answers. Why would someone abduct Edith? Obviously it wasn't only the driver of the green car, he was the errand boy, not the perpetrator behind it. Madame Lefarge had suggested he could be a local. Was he connected with the assailant from the other hotel? It was clear he had received instructions from another, or how and why had he picked on Edith? What did she have that someone else might benefit from, were it in his possession? What if Simon Markham were behind it? What could he want now?

Her last thoughts before her eyes closed with fatigue were that maybe Antoine would have been in touch with his colleagues overnight and have some answers tomorrow.

Chapter 15

The next morning Maree found Edith was first downstairs, brighter and much more her old self. The men arrived and they breakfasted together, postponing conversation until after they had eaten. Over a final cup of tea it was decided that there would be no travelling today. Grenoble had much to offer the visitor, and they would simply stroll around at leisure.

The weather appeared to be in their favour, cool and a little overcast. Ideal for a browse around the shops, lunch at one of the many pavement cafés, something they had not yet indulged in, and possibly take in a museum or art gallery for the afternoon. One thing was certain: they would stay together.

Maree also decided that it was time she rang Oaklands. She had promised to call them at the end of the first week. True, that was a couple of days away, but she wanted to let Matron know everything was all right. There was no need to tell her of Edith's worrying escapade; that would keep until their return.

Then Madame Lefarge came in to say, "The man with the green car is here to speak with the little lady." Maree's heart skipped a beat. Oh, not again, please, she begged silently.

Thankfully Antoine stood up. "Stay where you are, Edith. I will speak with him."

"Wait, please. He has come for his key." Edith pulled a large key from her bag.

"I think he would have to give this back to the man who gave it to him."

"Ah, good." Antoine nodded. "Now I might get some sense out of the man. Wait here all of you I will be as quick as I can."

Antoine followed the manageress out. The three of them sat and waited as he had requested. Maree had no idea how Edith was feeling, but her own heart was racing. Although she knew Edith was now safe, the thought of her captor being in such close proximity was enough to turn her legs to jelly. She wanted to put her arms around her friend, hold her close and shield her from anyone else getting near.

Treve sat next to Edith. As if he too felt the tension, he took her hand, smiling at her.

"Are you OK?" he asked.

Edith looked up with a grin. "I am all right now. I am with my friends. Antoine will soon send him packing. He will not trouble us again."

Maree prayed she was right.

The waitress came in and glanced at Edith, who spoke to her in French. The girl smiled and began clearing the table of the breakfast debris.

"Merci, remain safe Madame," she whispered to Edith as she left the room with her tray of dirty dishes.

Antoine returned. "All is well, my friends." He placed an arm across Edith's shoulder as he took his place at her side. "And you have made a conquest, dear Edith. That man has expressed great admiration for you. He said you must have the agility of a monkey to have got out of that building without doing yourself harm."

Edith looked at him. "I did not tell him that I keep fit and do exercises every day."

Antoine smiled at her. "No matter, he was happy with the key. Now he has gone. He will not come again."

"Are you sure of that, Antoine?" Treve asked. "We can travel with freedom for the remainder of our holiday?"

"Yes," Antoine smiled. "That fellow, he is called Marcel by the way, has told me that he did not know who paid him to pick up the lady from the hotel and that he will never do such a thing again."

"It doesn't solve the problem of who is behind the plot to abduct my aunt, does it?" Treve said. "Someone must have ordered the first man to do it. And why, I wonder, did Marcel not refuse to act on the other's bidding? He was not being forced, I take it?"

"Marcel does a little local taxi service as part-time employment," Antoine said. "He had no idea what that particular fare would involve him in. When the keys to the monastery were given to him it was by a female who did not speak but told him to read the note which was attached to them. Then she ran away. He had no way of contacting the man and refusing to pick up the fare. He genuinely expected the fellow to meet him at the property to explain what the fare had done to warrant being locked away".

"He thought I would tell him all he wanted to know," Edith butted in. "When I did not tell him what he expected, he said he wanted no part in it. Then he promised me the key if I would try to get out by myself."

"Which you did," Antoine said. "Now you are safe with us again we have to keep you that way until we return to England." He thought for a minute. "Well, there are three of us," he continued. "We are tall, strong adults. We have the advantage of being forewarned. Surely we can protect one dear friend from one man, whoever he is?"

Treve placed an arm protectively around Edith's shoulders. "I will not let her out of my sight. She must stay within my reach at all times."

"But what about the places you cannot go into, my brave

149

nephew?" Edith grinned at him. "You forget Treve, ladies have to visit their own powder rooms, and you would not be permitted to enter."

"Ah, but!" Treve laughed at her. "If I cannot go with you then no man can, so only ladies will be in those places."

"Well spoken, Treve," Antoine said. "Now if we are all ready, let us go out for a walk around Grenoble." As they left the dining room he whispered to Maree, "Don't worry, I will also be vigilant from now on."

The day passed pleasantly enough. Maree was uneasy when she twice saw a man who reminded her of Simon Markham and she felt vulnerable sitting in public view outside the busy café at lunchtime, but not wishing to disturb the general peace, she said nothing.

Over dinner Edith surprised them all by asking if anyone objected if she and Antoine went somewhere on their own for a few hours the next day.

Treve answered her. "Of course not Aunt, it is your holiday, you must do as you please."

Maree wondered what might be behind it. She hoped it wasn't because Edith was thinking it would be easier to go off on her own. Treve must have had similar ideas.

"As long as you are enjoying yourself, we have no objections," he said. "Just do not go off and leave Antoine to worry about you."

"I will not. I will stay with my friend the whole time," Edith promised.

The following morning, as Treve still had the maps to the Gorges, he and Maree set off on foot to explore as much of them as possible. They were unable to reach any great height, but the scenery from all the hairpin bends and the curves of the paths were spectacular. Cyclists, suitably clad in Lycra suits and crash helmets but, it seemed to Maree, only lightly equipped bicycle wise for what must be a strenuous ride further on, passed them with cheery greetings to 'Get yourselves bikes!'

She was surprised to note that the majority of the properties they could see in the distance were built of stone. She had expected chalet-type wooden buildings. Treve suggested it was possibly because the weather at that height was unpredictable. Chalets would not be warm enough in the colder air. They learned later, from a young English-speaking Hollander who joined their table at lunchtime, that many sports people stayed for long holidays. There were, Lief told them, ski resorts and many other facilities higher up. Every type of sport and leisure was catered for in the Alps. Climbing holidays or simple sightseeing from the cable cars brought thousands of people armed with backpacks, cameras and every type of sports equipment. He was an artist on a sketching holiday working from much higher up the mountain. Today he was on his way back up after taking some of his work down to be displayed and hopefully sold in a local market. He had chosen to walk for exercise.

Once he had left them they sat on, admiring the splendour all around and speculating on what the remainder of their time here in France might consist of. As it depended entirely on Edith, Maree was reminded of recent events and wondered how she and Antoine were doing. She hoped they were still together.

She needn't have concerned herself. When they met up again in the evening Antoine assured them he had left Edith for only a few minutes and even then she had been in his sights the whole time. Apparently she had wanted to visit her husband's memorial. She had not liked to suggest that they all accompanied her, for only Antoine had been present at the actual funeral. It had been considerate of her and he had readily agreed to go, leaving her only after paying his own respects at the graveside so that she could have a few private moments alone.

He had strolled around the paths of the cemetery and noted her meeting and conversation with a younger man. By the time he reached them she was already shaking hands in farewell. Although he did not ask who he was or offer to introduce him, she did enlighten him over lunch.

"The young man I was talking to is a nephew of Luc's. I have not seen him since he was about sixteen. He saw me get out of the car when you stopped outside the cemetery. He didn't know I had left France. He was puzzled why he did not see me around any more."

Edith told Maree some of this when they talked in her room before bed that evening.

"So will you keep in touch with him now, Edith?" she asked.

"No, he was at college when Luc had his accident and had just finished at university when he died. He would not have known his uncle. He would have been at home on holidays when he came sometimes with his parents to meet me at the solicitor's rooms. That's why he remembers me. Now he is a married man with family. We would have nothing in common."

Maree was thoughtful when she went to her own room, uneasy at the contact being renewed with Luc's family, who had caused Edith so much unhappiness before she came to Cornwall. She hoped they had not exchanged addresses. Probably not, she told herself. If they were not to keep in touch there would be no call to.

The next morning they talked of going to Strasbourg, but Edith surprised them by announcing that she was having second thoughts about visiting the area. She did however wish to go to Annecy. There was a particular château high above the fifteenth-century town where she had once gone with Luc to visit an elderly partially-sighted lady. This lady had been responsible for Luc obtaining a well-paid commission supplying maps for the whole of the Alpine lakes area, together with its mountain passes and adjoining towns and villages. While she did not expect the lady to still be living in the area, it was possible someone would be able to tell her where she could be found. She had to tell her of Luc's accident and that she was no longer living in France.

She remembered also that the castle was in the process of being renovated when she had last been in the area and thought that if it was now open to the public they could spend some time visiting it. Should that be unavailable to them, they could go on a boat ride around the lake, which she assured them was one of the prettiest of all the lake rides and should not be missed. Maree asked if they should be staying on in Grenoble or seeking another hotel in Annecy.

"The men can find us a hotel, I am sure," Edith said, directing a winning smile at Antoine and Treve.

So it was decided to move on to Annecy to stay for as long as they wished, once they'd established a base. The morning was spent repacking in preparation for the move in the afternoon.

Leaving the hotel was a long-winded affair. Madame Lefarge was concerned for Edith's welfare, begging them all to take great care of the little lady who had suffered so much. In vain did Edith protest that neither the man nor the experience had harmed her. Finally, by promising that if it could be arranged they would call in on their return journey, they left. Edith travelled with Antoine in his car, while Maree stayed with Treve in his.

Annecy itself excited Maree. The town at the head of the lake was busy, but with less of the noisy, bustling activity that was Grenoble. She guessed this was due to it being a holiday area as opposed to a study centre filled with a younger learning element. It was picturesque, with the castle looking down majestically over all, and it took only minutes for all of them to decide this was where they wanted to stay.

Gracious hotels interspersed with discreet private residences gave the lakeside a calm, peaceful atmosphere. Here and there a restaurant board advertised appetising meals and invited the public to try the menu. Small craft sailed quietly around the lake. Nothing large or noisy spoiled the charm. They learned from the small, tastefully-erected guide-boards which were discreetly dotted about on the grass verges that motorised craft were strictly monitored, with an almost apologetic explanation that this would ensure the lake would remain clean for agreeable, thoughtful people to continue to use.

They chose a small hotel to enquire for vacancies and while the men went in, Edith and Maree sat on a seat in the brilliantly flower-bedecked garden.

"This is lovely," Maree said. "What a contrast to Grenoble. Everything is so much quieter."

"Yes." Edith's voice was low, as if to raise it would cause noisy vibrations. "I did not come to Annecy many times when I lived in France before. But I wish to do so as I would have liked to sail in these." She shook her head gently, sighing, "Oh, such blue waters!"

"Does Antoine sail, Edith?"

"Only very little, he has no need, there are river police with their own fast boats. So the highway patrols have only the road traffic and pedestrians to attend to." She was thoughtful. "If we ask and the men are agreeable, we can hire a boat together with a strong man to pilot it. Then we will all have a holiday. That will be good. Do you not agree, Maree?"

"A very good idea, Edith. Maybe if that is not possible we could go for walks. I noticed some footpaths as we drove into the town, but I should also like to see the view from the top." Maree recalled the booklet with the picture of Annecy that Antoine had given her. "My book says you can also get good views of Mont Blanc and some of the more spectacular Alps from the castle." Silently she prayed nothing would happen this time to upset arrangements.

Antoine and Treve appeared from the hotel doorway.

"News! Ladies, the management has two double rooms

available," Treve announced. "It will mean you two sharing, and Antoine and I will take the other. The alternative is you each take one room and we will look for rooms in another hotel?"

"Oh no!" Maree let it slip without thinking how it might have sounded. It wasn't that she didn't want to share with Edith, but she was conscious of suddenly becoming responsible for looking after her on her own if the men were not nearby to help. She'd already given her the slip twice.

It was Edith who helped ease the situation.

"But what is wrong with those suggestions? If you do not mind sharing with each other then I think Maree and I can do so also. We shall be able to have the talks long into the night."

And so it was settled. Antoine and Treve went off to collect the cars from the car park they'd left them in while they sought accommodation. When they returned they were asked to park at the rear of the hotel. This was a satisfying location, to Maree's way of thinking, as the cars could not be seen from the road. She was still wary, and felt sure they had not heard the last of Simon Markham. If anyone was looking out for their cars, they wouldn't be easy to spot from behind the building.

Chapter 16

Their cases having been taken to their rooms, Edith and Maree spent the afternoon unpacking, showering and changing out of their travelling clothes in preparation for dinner. There was ample space in each room for two twin beds with a lot of space between them, one large wardrobe and a walk-in dressing room equipped with a small wardrobe. They had no difficulty stowing clothes.

When all was done, Edith clapped her hands excitedly.

"You see, we are well housed, are we not? We will be able to stay here for many days until we have seen all we wish to see in this lovely French town, and we are free to move around with the men to take care of us."

Maree guessed this must mean Edith too was thinking of staying safely in a group, so she would be reluctant to go off on her own. She breathed a sigh of relief. Hopefully they would all be able to enjoy the remainder of the holiday. She picked up the book which had accompanied the picture of Annecy and suggested they made their way to the lounge. Here they found Antoine and Treve already seated.

"Ah, our pretty ladies," said Antoine. He stood up, coming over to take Edith by the arm.

"Dinner will be in one hour, will you have a drink and sit with us here?"

Edith nodded, "A sweet sherry please."

"And you Maree?" Antoine smiled. "What will you have?"

Maree suddenly felt as though there were reasons to celebrate: staying in this lovely hotel, and the four of them together for what she hoped would be at least a week. A sense of peace stole over her. Tonight all was well. She would forget her usual iced water.

"The same for me please, Antoine."

The room was spacious and airy, with several double-seat settees and matching armchairs. Occasional tables were dotted about nearby. An electric piano stood at the far end, beside a casement window, its lid open as though its previous player had only just vacated the stool. Delicate watercolours of spring flowers graced the walls, and the room offered comfort. Placing her sherry on a nearby table, Maree sank gratefully on to the settee next to Treve, while Edith sat with Antoine. Far from relaxing, as Maree had proposed until dinner, Edith was full of life.

"This is beautiful, so much more like the holiday I had planned before we left Oaklands," said Edith. "There is much here for us to enjoy. We must arrange what we are to do tomorrow."

Oaklands! Hearing the word reminded Maree that she had not yet rung Matron. She must do so. Now though, she would sit here quietly, enjoying these moments of peace.

"Will this suit you for a few days?" Treve's hand grasped hers.

"Yes, Treve, thank you, it will more than do."

Dinner in the comfortable but lightly-furnished dining room, with a veranda overlooking the garden equipped with umbrella-shaded tables and chairs, was appetising and satisfying. All selected the same dishes; spring vegetable soup, noisettes of lamb, new potatoes, baby carrots and fresh garden peas, followed by a soft fruit salad accompanied by three varieties of cream.

EVE PARSONS

Choosing not to sit too long after it, they set off through the garden and on to the wide path around the end of the lake. The sight of the small craft sailing on the lake seemed to remind Edith of her suggestion earlier. When they found a seat in an excellent position to view most of the activities going on around them, she put a question to Antoine and Treve.

"Could we hire a strong man and his boat to take us on a tour around the lake while we are here in Annecy?"

"That sounds an attractive idea," Treve said happily. "I'd go along with that."

"It's a distinct possibility," said Antoine. "It's a busy time of year though, so we might have to book, specially if we require the services of a boatman as opposed to looking after ourselves. I suggest we call in at the offices tomorrow and check on what's involved. What about you, Maree, would you be happy to spend some time sailing?"

Maree was reluctant to admit that the only sailing she'd done was with Simon and a group of his sporting friends. As she didn't speak sailing language, she had usually spent the day close to the young man who had done the steering. He too had seemed a bit of a loner. To Antoine now, she merely smiled and agreed, hoping she wouldn't disgrace herself by falling overboard or even worse, suffer from sea-sickness.

Happy that her suggestion had gone down so well, Edith skipped along contentedly beside Antoine. When they reached some well-cared-for gardens, which at home would have been described as a park, Edith went off at a trot, dancing in and out of the trees like a six-year-old. Antoine laughed. To Treve he whispered, "She is a papillon!"

"Butterfly, he means," Treve said in Maree's ear.

"He's right," she replied. "She is like a butterfly today. But isn't it wonderful to have her back to normal?"

158

"Much more like herself, I agree. Let's hope she can stay that way."

Treve squeezed her arm. "I think we should have some time on our own. What do you say to us spending the evening together?"

"I'd love to Treve, but don't forget I'm supposed to be looking after Edith. I have already had a couple of frights. I don't want to be responsible for another."

"I'm sure Antoine will be only too pleased to look after her, and bear in mind she is an adult, it's not like having a child foisted on one."

"I know what you're saying. Providing neither of them object it's fine with me."

And of course they had no reason to disagree. Edith actually blamed herself for Maree not having had free time to shop or choose her own entertainment.

"You were supposed to have a holiday too, Maree. We've been here almost a whole week and I haven't been as good a guide as I promised I would be. I'll be accused of neglect. So you and Treve must now take care of each other." She smiled mischievously. "Antoine and I can explore Annecy together. We will visit the good lady friend of Luc in the château near the castle and find out if any of my theatre friends remain in the show business world of today."

Antoine seemed keen on the idea. "I suggest four or five days here in this perfect location, travelling back via Provence, then on our arrival at the coast in some days we can spend time together visiting the Roman museums and artefacts we avoided when we first arrived in France."

"And we'll go to the beach and paddle in the sea like schoolchildren," Edith giggled, grasping Maree's hand. "We have not yet used our bathing costumes, or our evening frocks. Ah!" She sighed. "I have been at fault I think, now we must make it up. This week shall be a real holiday. Treve will show you, Maree, what France has to offer young people such as yourselves."

Treve held her hand. "I'm sure we will find something you will enjoy," he said quietly. "Please, please agree."

Maree smiled up at him, "I very much look forward to seeing France through your eyes, Treve, that is provided Edith is enjoying her holidays too."

The next morning, breakfast over, they went together to the offices alongside the lake and made enquiries regarding a boat and a man to take them out for a trip.

"This is a busy holiday time," said the man in the office. "There are no boats with men available until tomorrow. You could have a boat only for a few hours today if you wish, but with someone to take the wheel you should book today." So after consultation Antoine booked a four-hour session the following morning. The two couples then went their separate ways.

Treve and Maree wandered through the fifteenth-century streets and shopping centre, and were very impressed by the ancient architecture and the way modern renovation has been skilfully blended in. Here there were fashion houses of the highest repute, where it was still the practice to put only one example of a particular designer's quality work into the shop window. Matching accessories accompanied it. Price tickets were not visible. Recalling her nursing friend's philosophy, 'if you have to ask the price you cannot afford it,' Maree turned away.

Pâtisseries were popular, and the appetising smells of croissants and pastries wafted along every street. It wasn't difficult to discover their source. The assortment of people queuing for these food items represented all walks of life. Many were obviously tourists intent on having a good time. The laughter and jollity exhibited, though only in a shopping queue together, brought smiles to other faces too.

They decided on a crêperie for lunch. Never having had pancakes except on Shrove Tuesday, Maree tucked into hers with relish. It was delicious. She chose runny golden syrup and ice cream as the filling, unusual in France, but the waitress did not demur over the strange request. It was literally a melt in the mouth experience. She came away with mind made up; she must ask her mother to teach her to make them when she next got home for more than a couple of days.

Treve had selected soft fruits, raspberries and redcurrants with a pouring cream. A sample taste told her it was sharper on the palate, but would be just as nice, depending on what you'd eaten before it.

They followed lunch with a stroll through a well-laid-out garden. A seat in the shade was next on the itinerary, and they found one beneath a large plane tree. A mother duck and her young brood of nine ducklings pecked away in the grass nearby. Although there was no water that they could see, Maree could hear a moorhen calling. The lake was obviously close. She began to thinking about the coming boat trip the next day.

"Penny for them," Treve whispered.

"I'm wondering about tomorrow's boat trip," she murmured. "I'm not sure about it."

"Have you not sailed before?" Treve took her hand. "We'll call it off if you'd rather not go."

"Yes, I have sailed, several times, but they were experiences best forgotten."

"Then we must ensure that such memories are not repeated. You will stay close to me. I will personally see to it that you're cared for." He placed a finger under her chin, forcing her to look up at him. "Remember, if you feel too uncomfortable we can ask to be put ashore at any time. Antoine and Edith can still go on with the trip."

"Will it be much different from going out to sea? I have never sailed on a lake before. Do we have to sit still all the time?"

"It will be quite different. For a start there will be no large boats close by, so no washes coming to upset our calm waters. No noisy or smelly engines discharging black oil in the water. As for moving about, we will be offered refreshments. We can stand at the rail to eat or remain seated. A lot will depend on the skipper."

"Will he talk to us? Or will he be concentrating only on the steering?"

"Most of them are friendly. He will be pointing out important sites of interest, mainly on the land, as we pass. Some of the boat owners actually go closer in shore to show us picturesque places which are not clear enough from further out."

"Do we ask for this service, or is it something the skipper decides to do?"

"You can ask, but it's up to the skipper. Occasionally if things are going well they will even pull in to a quayside where a small market might be selling fresh produce or hand crafted gifts. People like us are often only too pleased to take home goods they can't buy in the shops."

"It all sounds interesting Treve, I know I'm going to enjoy the day."

"If I have anything to do with it you will."

And enjoy it she did. The whole trip was a smooth, comfortable ride, from the beginning, when the boatman helped them aboard, to when they clambered out at the landing stage at lunchtime.

They did go ashore, like many other boating visitors, to purchase gifts to take home. Edith discovered one studio selling handheld fans and feather boas, which were second-hand but all appeared of good quality. She was excited, dragging Maree by the hand to help her choose which to buy.

Maree bought handmade lace and embroidered table linen. Having seen so much of it while they'd been travelling, she knew she could never explain the beauty of it to her mother. She thought Matron too would appreciate a tablecloth with runner to match.

For Barbara she settled on a hand-decorated porcelain

photograph frame. Edith had given her a copy of each of the photos she'd had taken with Mum and Dad at the vicarage. Barbara was more likely to put a picture of her parents on display if she had a nice frame for it. She added another frame enclosing a picture of Lake Geneva to the bag for Val.

Picturesque calendars for the coming year also ended up among Maree's gifts, enough for all the staff and residents at Oaklands. It truly had been a lovely day, and she mused, who wouldn't enjoy it with such attentive escorts? Though they'd had to put up with a bit of leg-pulling from the men, suggesting the boat might not make it back to base with all the extra weight they'd brought on board. Luckily, having bought flat packages, there was no problem stowing them in the suitcases on their return to the hotel.

Next day Treve and Maree chose to leave the car and walk along the lakeside. A superbly sited nearby town is pretty and elegant Talloires. Although somewhat crowded with hotels and restaurants, from it one gets beautiful views across Lake Annecy, which, they were informed, is at its narrowest here. They discovered a castle in the water at the foot of a mountain range and learned later it was named Duingt's and the range Taillefer Ridge.

After dinner that evening they studied the information leaflet again and thought that the following day they might drive through the woods to the other side of the Ridge and take photographs of the Alps from a different angle. The hotel owner assured them they would not regret the experience. There were good walking paths, she said, but to be sure to wear stout shoes. She also agreed to packing them a picnic lunch, normal procedure for the guests from her hotel, she emphasised.

Edith and Antoine arrived after dinner, having also had a satisfying day. They had managed to find the whereabouts of her old friend, who had in turn passed on the address of a former theatre lady dresser. When they learned she was still resident in Lyon, arrangements were made to visit her the next day. Maree was delighted that Edith had found someone associated with her happier years in France.

It appeared that none of the other guests staying in the hotel wished to remain in the lounge for the evening, and as the four of them wanted no more of the great outdoors for the day, they sat on exchanging their experiences and making plans for the next day. Maree and Edith talked very little that night; they fell into bed and slept the sleep of the just.

The following morning they woke refreshed and well prepared for whatever the day held. The drive from the west bank of the lake up through the wooded Semnoz Mountain was so extraordinary in places that it literally took their breath away, making them gasp in wonder. How they wished they'd had a cine camera. As it was, they contented themselves with stopping at every convenient spot to take still shots on their digital cameras. The crags of La Tournette towered over them.

Looking it up in the guidebook while enjoying the picnic lunch, they were not surprised to learn that the crags were over two thousand three hundred metres high and some of the roads higher up had to be closed for weeks in the winter.

Knowing this was to be their last day in Annecy made it all the sweeter, and they resolved that it was another of the areas they would definitely revisit when possible.

Returning early, Maree rang Oaklands on the hotel phone. She found it surprisingly easy to get through. The line was clear and devoid of crackle. Matron was pleased. She'd heard nothing more about the break-in and there'd been no more problems. Maree made no mention of Simon or Antoine. After assuring her that they were enjoying themselves and she'd save details until they returned, she said goodbye. She spent time repacking before showering. This, she felt, would give Edith more space to get her own repacking done.

Once again they dined in the hotel without Edith and Antoine, who did not return until eight o'clock in the evening. It transpired they had spent nearly all day in Fourvière, near Lyon, with her old friend the theatre dresser. The lady had been delighted to see Edith after so many years. They'd had much news to catch up on and finally decided to go out for a meal when it was too late to get back in time for dinner at the hotel.

One other piece of news Edith hastened to tell them. They had met Simon Markham. He had apparently been cruising with friends in his own boat, which was moored on the river close by. He had been accompanied by one of those friends, a young lady named Nina. This had not prevented Edith from asking a question.

"He says it was not him who pushed me into the garden at the hotel that first evening," she told them. "He says he did not stop after the ferry docked, but went on to pick up his friends in Nice."

"So we are not likely to solve that particular mystery then?" Maree remarked.

"It must have been an accident," Antoine said. "Some visitor in a hurry. Best to forget it ever happened. Now let us change the subject. I take it we are still of one mind, that we move on to Provence tomorrow?"

They were all in agreement, so they sat on for some time in the lounge poring over the map, choosing the route that would take them to Provence without retracing the previous journey. Eventually they decided to head for St-Jean-de-Maurienne, with possibly a stop off at Albertville, a town used in the 1992 Winter Olympics, and still showing evidence of it. Then they would go on to Aix-en-Provence. Next stop, the coast.

That settled, the ladies retired to bed, where Maree, who was feeling a little under the weather and thought she might be coming down with a cold, was content to listen to Edith relating what her day's activities had involved. Some of their time had been spent in the museum of silk and costumes, which the men and Maree had visited on the day Edith had not been with them. This news pleased Maree.

It transpired that there was little to see in Albertville, apart from a display of sports costume videos if you were prepared to spend the time viewing, together with photographs of some of the Olympic events. Nearby they discovered the town of Conflans, beautifully restored and turned into a busy area of craft shops. In most of them work was being demonstrated. Much of it could be bought, and they would have taken advantage of this if they had not purchased so many gifts already.

But here in one of the cafés, they met Simon. He was smiling to himself as he strode away. He did not even say goodbye. Dismay registered on Treve's face as he stared after the man before turning to his aunt. "You should not have told him what our future plans are, Aunt Edith."

"But he is concerned with Maree not being with us today, Treve. What would you have me do? Tell him to mind his own business?"

"Yes, she has only a cold and sits in the garden today, she will soon be over it. She dislikes him intensely. Their engagement finished a long time ago. It will upset her more if he goes around making a nuisance of himself."

Edith was unsure. Maree would think it was her fault. She was not aware that Maree and that man Simon had been engaged before she met him. Why did he not mention it? Why did they finish it? And why was he pretending they were still betrothed? Now she was confused.

She got into the car. Treve did not speak for a long time, so she thought about the problem.

Edith remembered the first time she had seen Simon Markham. He was in the side garden at Oaklands when she had come out to do her exercises. When he saw her he was going to turn back to the rear. She'd asked him if he was looking for someone particular and if she could help him. She recalled how startled he seemed; he looked as if he would run away. Then he asked for someone whose name she did not recognise. When she had said there was no one of that name living at Oaklands, he had left.

It had occupied her thoughts for many days afterwards. She wondered why he had not come to the front door and asked for the lady he was seeking. She had met him again in the town one day when she had been shopping and he had insisted on buying her a coffee. Since then he had called on her at Oaklands or arranged to meet her in the city. But up to now, as far as she could recall, he had not spoken of Maree.

She would have to speak with Antoine. He was a wise man; he would help clear her mind of the troubles.

To give Maree a couple of days to recover, they made up their minds to remain at Gap. They intend spending time walking alongside the lake, the west side of which was quiet and gave a good view of what are known as the Bonneted Maidens, pillars of soft rock which have somehow been saved from too much erosion by a small boulder still sitting on the top.

When they walked Antoine and Treve took photographs, revelling in the colours of everything around them. South of the Savines, a small lakeside resort, is a forest. The area is inhabited by chamois, though they are extremely elusive animals and they were disappointed not to see any. The leaves of the trees had started to display the autumn reds and oranges. The stonework of the buildings, especially the hotel they are staying in, also appeals to them.

They came upon a pass that made a spectacular picture, with red treetops in the foreground, grey and blue crags of the mountains behind, with white peaks of snow and above it all, the bluest of blue sky. "Such a beautiful picture it makes!" Edith felt compelled to say to them.

Another beautiful picture came to mind, as she recalled later to Antoine. "Maree and Treve, I believe they are attracted to each other," she said. "They do not know I see, but he shows much concern for her welfare. It would be a pleasant situation if they became a couple in love".

"You would like for such a happening while we are on holiday Edith?"

"Yes, we could have much celebrations. I do not understand why she has no special male friend in Cornwall. She is a caring and helpful young woman, and I believe she will make an adoring wife to the right man, who could be my nephew Treve. I wish them both to be happy, Antoine."

That night when they had finished dinner, two policemen arrived to speak with Antoine. When they had talked to him for a short while, they asked for Treve and Edith. They had notebooks and asked lots of questions, such as, "Who are you? Why have you come to France? Why have you travelled to so many places? How long do you plan on staying in the area?" They did not seem happy with the replies, and said they would have to talk to them again.

Antoine had an explanation when Treve told him. "Did you tell him about your abduction?" Antoine asked Edith.

"No, of course not and they did not ask. I was not hurt and you must remember the man who took me away was kind to me."

"I can see what Antoine is getting at, Aunt," Treve told her. "If someone or some persons are out to do us harm, why? The police are naturally suspicious that we might involve their forces in problems of our own making and are bringing trouble into France. How are they treating you, Antoine?"

"I do not fare much better than you, Treve, they are also suspicious of me."

"But you are a member of the French police! Surely they trust you?"

"I am not of their precinct, Treve. It takes a long time to become completely accepted into the whole unit, and you must remember I am not a Frenchman. The combined force is protective of its own."

"There goes that oaf Markham, not hanging around today I notice," Treve pointed to the car park exit. He and Edith were window shopping while Antoine visited the local precinct and Maree sat in the hotel garden warming herself, her cold almost cleared.

"Yes, I saw the red car." Edith nodded. "I think it is him with his water nymph. I hoped he would not be stopping today, to maybe cause us more trouble. Perhaps he leaves us now to sail away into the distance."

"Let's hope so. I can't think what he wants."

"He is just being a silly nuisance. He wishes only to aggravate you, Treve."

"You did not know he was once engaged to Maree then, Aunt? Maree has never confided in you?"

"No, but why should she? We do not have many opportunities for private talks, most of the time she is anxious to return to her work and sometimes another of the staff at Oaklands also comes with her. One day soon I hope she will come alone and we will talk about the theatre. I have promised to show my photographs of the days when I was in France. She has promised she will come when it is her day off from the house duties."

"I too would like to know more of those days. My mother said you very much enjoyed that period of your life. Whenever she returned from visiting you she said you were on top of the world and the theatre would be packed for the shows you were playing in. Did you really love your work?"

They came to a café with tables vacant outside.

"Shall we sit for a coffee?" said Treve.

"Yes please." Edith was grateful for the break from walking. When Treve returned with coffee for them both he requested she continue.

"It did not seem so much like work. Until Luc and I married I had nothing to do with my life except my acting and singing. I adored it, and the troupe I performed with were all happy people. New shows would be written with much fun for everyone to enjoy. It was a time of plenty in the theatre. We did not have to beg for anything."

"And what about the general public? Did they appreciate the theatre as much as the folk in Paris?"

"Lyon is France's second city. It too had wonderful theatres, as some of the museums now will prove to all of the world with their beautiful exhibits. Audiences flocked in for each performance. We had many prominent stars pleading to be given roles in our shows. The ticket sales were so good the managers often took us out for meals after a performance that pleased them. Those were good times."

"It sounds as if you and the theatre are well suited, Aunt. Have you ever thought of going back to it? There are many entertainment outlets in Cornwall, I understand. Choirs are popular and I believe you even have drama groups in nearly every town."

"I am trying, Treve. I have been in touch with some of the right people, now I wait to hear from them."

Treve took her hand in his. "I am pleased for you, Aunt," he said. "I hope you will not have to wait too long. And here is Antoine."

Chapter 17

Antoine made it clear he had something important to talk to Edith about. Treve had left them for an errand of his own.

"I have been doing some investigations into Simon Markham's background," he said.

"Oh, Antoine, is it safe that you do this? He can be a very angry man."

"I do not expect him to find out, Edith. I will not be telling anyone other than you. You will not mention it to him, I know."

Edith shook her head. "Of course I will say nothing to anyone. But why would you need to do it?"

"I am suspicious of him being in the same place as we are on so many occasions. I could not understand why he too needed to be there."

"But, Antoine, do you not remember the lady friend, her name is Nina, she accompanied him when we went to the village near Lyon?"

"Yes I remember, she was a boating friend."

"He tells me her sister works at the hospital. He wished her to know they would be going to the coast."

"I know that is what he tells you, Edith, but did you see this sister? No, I do not think you did."

Edith nodded in agreement. "It is true, I did not see this other person." She picked up her coffee, sipping it slowly while he talked.

"I found other things I do not care for, Edith, and I would ask that you be very careful in your dealings with him."

"Oh, are you going to tell me of them?"

Antoine drank his own coffee thoughtfully. He was reluctant to enlighten her on all he had discovered. He had planned on telling Treve only, and that simply so that he could protect Maree.

"I will say only that you must have nothing to do with him, especially concerning finances. Markham has robbed the family business by taking money that he is not entitled to. His father has now put a stop on future withdrawals outside England, so it could be that he will have to look elsewhere for money."

"But I do not think he would ask me for it, Antoine. I agree with you it is not a nice thing to take what does not belong to you, but who would tell you of such things? Was it his father?"

"You should know better than expect me to tell you of my source, Edith. You must take my word for it, he is not someone you should be friendly with. If you see him again try not to be alone with him."

"He has asked me to go on a trip in his boat. Are you making a suggestion I should say no to him? I do not think I would have a good reason to give him. He would not wish to hurt me, and if I do not talk about money I should be safe. Do you not agree? After all, he says he was not in the area when I was pushed down the steps of the hotel. He could be telling the truth."

He knew he was not getting through to her. "But don't you see?" He took her hand in his, anxious that she should understand his concern. "Edith my dear, once again you are having to take his word for truth."

"What you say is true, Antoine, but I have never before discovered him to be telling me lies."

"Have you ever checked on something he has told you? Made enquiries about him?"

"No," she replied thoughtfully. "But I think to myself he is solicitor, he should be truthful in all of his statements." She shrugged. "So I must do as you say and be extra careful if he comes to see me again."

"It is best you do not talk with him. If he does turn up again you must definitely say nothing of what we have discussed, and another thing, you should not even consider going on his boat. I am sure that Treve will agree with me and also say you should keep your feet firmly on dry land." He looked up, smiling. "Here comes Treve."

"I guessed you might still be here," said Treve. He joined them at the table, sitting next to Antoine.

That night while Maree showered, Edith, prepared for bed but not yet sleepy, sat beside the open window and fell to thinking about what Antoine had told her he had learned about Simon. Up to now she had been of the opinion that Simon was being unfairly regarded by the others. She was still sure it was he who had pushed her down the hotel steps on her first night back in France. She was even more certain it had been a deliberate push. Supposing though, it was not herself he had meant to hurt? Maybe there was someone else he had a grudge against. And if, as Treve and Antoine were saying, he had been engaged to Maree and she had broken the engagement off...

Oh, but to deliberately hurt a woman! Especially one he was supposed to have loved. That would make him a dreadfully nasty man. She wasn't sure she could think of him like that. Although, if he had stolen from his father's firm, it seemed there was indeed something dubious about him. Oh dear! This was getting her nowhere.

She rose from the chair, drank from the glass of water she had beside the bed and climbed back in. Maree returned, and they settled down. Soon Maree's gentle breathing told her that her friend would not be telling her anything tonight, but sleep still eluded her. Tossing and turning she made up her mind that she herself would resolve the problem. She must trust that Maree would have something to say when she enquired from her about the relationship. After all, if she had been close to the man, she would know him better than the rest of them.

Over breakfast the next morning they talked over what they might do to finish the holiday off in an appropriate manner. Edith suggested that they should stick to their original plan, head for the coast and spend the last few days in a quiet hamlet. Leaving the friendly guest house in the small town of Gap, they travelled in their two cars, Treve working hard to prove how well he was going to take care of his passenger, in spite of Maree's protestations that he was wrapping her up like one of his precious relics. Having arranged that should they become separated whilst driving, they would meet up in Aix-en-Provence, they thankfully arrived without incident.

It was soon agreed they would spend a couple of days at least in this spa town. Antoine knew a little of its history and assured them that in spite of it being a university town it would be suitable for the relaxing pleasures they hoped to enjoy.

Visiting the Granet Museum, they spent the afternoon viewing works of antique sculptures and paintings by artists representing many countries. Still intent on travelling back to the ferry via the coast, the next day they headed for Marseille, but the nearer they got to the large port the more crowded the route became. When they eventually found a car park and studied the map they looked for smaller ports and harbours. Finally they chose Sète, and moved on. When that area too proved to be distinguished only for its water sports, they stayed only long enough to eat in one of the many fine fish restaurants before moving on to Agde.

Here they learned that Agde is a much older port than Sète. It stands on the bank of the river Hérault, not far from the mouth. Of Greek origin, the name is believed to be derived from Agatha. It boasts a small crenellated cathedral, and an archaeological museum built from dark volcanic stone, making it less interesting than other buildings. This suited the four of them, who were grateful for the quieter, less frenetic situation. Antoine as usual found them lodgings on the outskirts of town.

Chapter 18

Two days into their stay they opted for a drive to the local marina and a walk along the sea front. The last person they were thinking of, or expected to meet, was Simon Markham. But meet him they did.

Simon appeared pleased to see them, showing no signs of the animosity of the last time they had met, and seemed genuinely interested in Maree's health without enthusing over her too eagerly. Most of his attention and charm was focused on Edith.

"I hope you haven't forgotten the jaunt on my boat we'd planned, Edith?" he said. "We must arrange something now we've met at last. How long are you staying here?"

Edith was a little put out by Simon mentioning the boat viewing as if it had been definitely arranged when in fact she had promised nothing, and she was hesitant in replying. She glanced at Antoine.

"How long will we stay here, Antoine? Not for long, do you think?"

"No, a couple of days only my dear. Why? Have you made arrangements to visit somewhere?"

Simon's question came before Edith could reply. "Is Edith not free to go out alone then?"

Antoine laughed. "Of course, Edith can please herself where she goes. But we are a foursome and wish to go around together. Treve and I take great pleasure in caring for our ladies, is that not so Treve?"

Simon smirked, placing an arm around Edith's shoulders. "Even so, if she is with me - I should, of course, say with us." He drew Edith closer, smiling down at her. "You remember Nina, Edith? She will also be aboard, so there will be two of us taking special care of you." He glanced up at Antoine. "So have no concerns my friend. Oh, and before you suggest otherwise, my cruiser is not large enough for you all."

Edith sensed that Simon was trying to provoke another scene. She hastened to calm the situation.

"Where is your boat tied up, Simon? I could think about coming for a short visit if I know where to find it."

Simon took her arm and turned her to face the inner harbour, which was filled with craft of all shapes and sizes.

"Do you see the row of motor cruisers far over close to the wall near the exit?"

Edith shaded her eyes.

"You must mean the ones without the tall masts? And the shiny rails all round them?"

"That's right. Mine is the one at the end of the row, the *Maxine Louise*."

"Then it must be the white one with the blue windows on top. Does it have a seat around beside the rails?"

"Yes, it is the white one with the blue wheelhouse, and she does have a seat all round outside with a safety rail, so no need to remain inside if you'd prefer not to. Now, if you give me a time, and I suggest you make it early in the morning so as not to waste the day, I could meet you here on this same spot."

Edith showed some anxiety. "It is safe to go outside the calm waters is it Simon? Do I have to wear a lifebelt all the time?"

"You need only wear your lifejacket when you are up top, Edith."

"Is your boat suitable for sea cruises or river trips only?" Antoine queried.

"It is capable of offshore cruising, which of course I take full advantage of, specially when I have guests aboard."

"Are you planning to go out of the marina seaward or just a trip up the river while Edith is with you?" Antoine asked.

"It's no business of yours," Simon replied sharply. "But since you ask, we might take a cruise. It will depend on what my two guests wish when we've talked together." He squeezed Edith's shoulders. "But there are far more interesting sights along the shoreline." He turned Edith to face himself. "What about it, will you come? Tomorrow maybe?"

Edith gave Maree an enquiring look, then asked quietly, "Will you be well enough for me to leave you in the care of these two gentlemen?"

Maree was hesitant in her reply. "I don't know," she said. "We have planned to stay together for the last week, and I'd rather you were close by Edith, in case I need your help." She sighed. "But I suppose the men and I can spend the morning browsing in the shops and pick you up again in time for lunch, if you must go."

"But I thought you ladies were shopping together during these last few days?" Antoine asked.

Edith glanced at Simon. "I too have some shopping to do, but only for a few personal items. I will do it before I arrive here." Wriggling out from under Simon's arm, she touched Antoine's hand. "Will that be all right? Will you come back for me at one o'clock?"

"Of course," Antoine said, before glancing sternly at Simon. "I trust your host will get you back on shore by then."

Treve took her hand. "What can I say, Aunt? I would prefer we all stayed together as planned. But don't forget, we'll be close at hand and watching from the harbour entrance. You must keep your eye on the time and remind your friend if he looks like running over time."

"That will depend where we are at the time," Simon grumbled. "If we're near the fort it could be inconvenient. It's rough water out there and rocky below, it makes turning about difficult. We could find it more convenient to motor further out to sea before turning..."

"I hope that doesn't make you later getting in," Antoine interrupted. "We shall be delaying lunch until Edith returns."

"I think you should go ahead and eat when you're ready," Simon said. "Edith might wish to remain on board. She doesn't realise of course how much pleasure she can gain from a motor cruiser, especially a thirty-footer with a competent skipper at the helm." Putting an arm around Edith's shoulders, he said, "But she will, she will." He turned away. "Oh well, that's it then. I'll see you here tomorrow morning."

Over lunch in one of the well-equipped restaurants, Maree asked Edith if she was sure she wanted to go with Simon and his girlfriend. Edith did not hesitate over her reply.

"I would much rather stay with you, Maree. We have missed many days of our holiday, we have much to make up. But I am thinking perhaps he will not harass us any more if I go with him this time."

Treve interrupted at this point. "Aunt Edith, you do not have to go, you must not allow him to browbeat you into doing something you'd rather not do. Antoine and I will have a word with him if you wish."

"Edith, we are your friends, he is not a good man for you to be dealing with," said Antoine. "You should forget the idea of going on his boat." He looked helplessly at the others. "We'd all be much

happier if you'd change the arrangements and remain with us."
She smiled at him. "When first we met in Lyon you saved me from
some amorous young men, and now you would save me again! But
we are so much older. I do not think this man Simon has the same
intentions towards me, do you?"

The others were busy with their own thoughts and none of
them answered. Tension mounted gradually between them as the
day continued. It had not eased when they retired to bed.

When they met at breakfast the next morning, Edith made it clear
they had not persuaded her to think again, but she promised to be
extra careful in moving about the boat and continually note the
time.

Soon the four of them were back at the harbour. Edith was
dressed in a bright turquoise trouser suit, white cardigan and a
white scarf tied loosely round her neck, white cap set jauntily on
her head. Maree remarked on how well she would stand out when
viewed through a telescope from the shore. Treve and Antoine,
equipped with cameras, were putting them to practical use taking
pictures of the harbour and boats at their moorings, including the
Maxine Louise.

Antoine sported a hefty pair of binoculars around his neck. He
looked at Edith now and asked "Is the white cardigan significant?"

Edith nodded. "I am pleased you take note of it Antoine, it
means you have not forgotten our little arrangement from a long
time ago."

He took her hand, looked down at her sternly and proceeded
to warn her once again. "You are making a grave mistake, Edith.
Why will you not heed our warnings? That man is bad news, he
has no thought for anyone other than himself." He turned her to
face the others. "You will have to be on the alert the whole time."

When Simon and his girlfriend Nina appeared they were
surprised to discover Edith had already arrived.

"Come aboard, Edith," Simon called as he climbed the iron ladder to join them. "It's such a lovely morning we won't waste a minute putting out to sea." He nodded to the others, grasping Edith by the arm. "Have you ever clambered down one of these before? No?" Edith was shaking her head. "Well, don't be afraid, I'll go ahead and be there to catch you if you fall." He laughed, seeming not to notice Edith's apprehension. But her friends did.

"Be careful, Edith," they chorused, stepping forward.

"You can still change your mind," Treve said quietly.

"Please don't fuss," Edith said, adding in a whisper for Treve's ears only, "It's not my first time on a boat, remember." Then loudly for the benefit of the others, "I will be quite all right once I have negotiated this cold ladder."

Once on board the *Maxine Louise*, Simon disappeared into what Edith knew to be the wheelhouse. As she followed Nina through a door and down three steps to a small, comfortable-looking seating area, she heard the engine start up. Within seconds they were under way.

"Oh, how cosy!" she murmured to Nina. "There is much more room than I imagined. Oops!" She almost fell sideways. "I will have to find some sea legs from somewhere, won't I?"

"Too right," Nina told her coldly. "We haven't had breakfast yet and you, missus, are going to have the privilege of getting it for us, so the quicker you find your sea legs the better."

Edith, though shocked at the venom in the girl's voice, was quick to reply as she sat in one of the two other seats on the opposite side of the cabin. "I was under the impression that this was Simon's boat. I don't think he would expect one of his guests to wait on other able people? Especially in the kitchen."

"Galley, you silly cow, it's called a galley not a kitchen," the girl sneered. "As for Simon, he'll be down here soon looking for food 'cos, like me he's only had the hair of the dog this morning so you'd better get moving."

"A hair of a dog?" Edith queried, "I do not understand this meal."

Nina shook her head at Edith disbelievingly. "You really are stupid aren't you? "The hair of the dog is another drink, woman. Having wine in the morning after drinking alcohol the night before is not good. So jump to it, we need food now, at once."

Edith had no intention of following the orders of this slip of a girl. At the same time she wondered what Simon and his guests normally did about meals. Perhaps they went ashore, though buying three meals a day would prove expensive. She mused on this for a while.

Nina was still curled up on the couch she'd thrown herself into on arrival. A sturdy little couch, resembling a chaise longue, the back was made up with short polished railings reaching from the padded curved head end to the foot that flattened out. It wouldn't do for a tall person, Edith decided.

Edith felt certain she was still being glared at from across the small cabin. She was determined not to move. Then it occurred to her that there was nothing to prevent her from going to see Simon. He had promised her she would enjoy the sea trip, and she couldn't do that if she was cooped up down here. She was also aware that if she joined him in the wheelhouse he could point out places of interest, as he'd promised. Shouldering her bag, she left the fractious Nina to her own devices.

Simon showed no animosity when Edith appeared in the entrance. In fact he seemed pleased to see her. "So, Edith, what do you think of my home on the water?" he asked.

"I'd like to know more about it, Simon. Do you truly live on it? It's very small compared to a house on the land isn't it?"

"It's compact, Edith, which suits a bachelor like me. It's easy to clean." He turned her, guiding her on to the deck. "And, if like today I'm entertaining, I can drop anchor for a while."

"What do you mean? Stop it? Leave it to go on its own? What if another boat came too close? Would you not collide?"

"Not at all, my dear, now, cast your eyes seaward. What can you see beyond those rocks?"

Edith did as he bid. "Maybe it would be a lighthouse?"

"And what else can you see?"

"It looks like a small castle." She nodded. "Yes it is, but why would anyone build a castle at sea? It is a long way out."

"It is not a castle, Edith, it is a fort, or what remains of one. Originally there was also a lighthouse standing beside it. Look again, can you see a short white tower?"

"Yes, it has a red lamp house and some little detached buildings."

"Those were cells."

"Does it have a name?" Edith asked. "Perhaps I can get a postcard picture of it to show my friends."

"Yes, its name is Fort Brescou. It is now a local sightseeing spot for boat trippers, although not as many go there in these days. Perhaps we will make time to go out there."

"This is a pleasant way to view the area." Edith smiled up at him. "I have never travelled on the sea before. I look forward to what other places you have to show me."

"Well, before we make too many plans, what about a coffee? You go and see Nina, she would like one I'm sure. You can tell her the ship's captain would like some refreshment, breakfast would be welcomed."

"Right sir," Edith agreed, whilst silently murmuring under her breath. "You'll be lucky, that young lady looks after number one only."

Nina, her head buried in a magazine, didn't look up when Edith returned and issued Simon's request.

"The captain asks me to tell you he would like some breakfast, if you please."

"Oh he would, would he?" Now she did look up, glaring dislike at Edith. "Then he can come and get it himself. I am not a servant." She turned another page of the magazine. "In any case he's supposed to be entertaining me, and that's what he did till you came on board."

"Perhaps I can help, I could make us coffee," Edith tentatively offered. "If you show me where to find the necessary ingredients."

"Through there." Raising her right hand, the ungracious Nina indicated a dark curtain hanging at the end of the couch she occupied. When Edith pulled it to one side, she discovered that it hid the entrance to the galley. Stepping through it and letting the curtain drop behind her she noticed a narrow door in the wall on her right. She was about to pull on the small handle, thinking to open it, when the girl's voice startled her.

"Take your nose out of that. What you're looking for is through there." She pushed Edith in the back, causing her to stumble into the tiny galley.

"It is not necessary to be forceful. You will not get the coffee any quicker," Edith protested.

Edith, narrowly avoiding a little table in the centre of the room, straightened up as she reached the small cooker with a cupboard next to it. On top of this stood an even smaller refrigerator. It contained bottles of milk and fruit juices, together with a small selection of dairy products. On the top shelf of the cupboard were cereals, bread and preserves. Below were dishes and a tray of cutlery. Leaving both doors open, she stood back to let the girl see what they contained.

"What do you want to eat?" she asked Nina.

"Cereals, toast and coffee. Simon will have the same." She turned away. "And be quick about it. We have other important things for you to do."

Edith filled the kettle. While it boiled she hunted around for trays. Going back to the cupboard she had uncovered behind the curtain earlier, she quietly eased the door open.

There on a shelf was her missing fan cabinet.

With difficulty she withheld the cry that sprang to her lips. After examining it quickly to make sure it was indeed her own cabinet, she quietly closed the door and crept back to the galley.

Her mind busy, she searched for, and eventually found, two trays. Placing them on the table, she asked herself what her cabinet could be doing here on Simon's boat. How could she open it to discover if her precious fans, especially the Leaf, were still inside? She was still convinced of Simon's involvement in her fall down the hotel steps, but what were his reasons for it? She could think of nothing she'd done to warrant his wishing to hurt her.

Moments later the trays each contained a full dish of sugar-coated cereal. Had someone examined them closely, they might have noticed that there was a little extra ingredient added to each, a fine powdered substance. They were accompanied by a jug of milk, a small jar of preserve and a couple of small pats of butter. Edith's purse was minus four painkillers.

While the toast was browning under the grill she prepared the mugs with coffee and added the boiled water.

"Get a move on in there, what's taking you so long?" Nina's whinging voice came just as Edith was rescuing the toast before it burned. Hurriedly placing it on a couple of plates, she added the cutlery and carried one tray into Nina.

"About time too, I told you to move it." The ungrateful girl almost snatched the tray as, careful not to spill any of its contents Edith handed it to her, returning to the galley to collect the remaining one for Simon.

"And come straight back," Nina called after Edith as she passed, "I shall want more coffee."

Edith did not reply but carried on to give Simon his breakfast, without telling him who had prepared it.

"This looks good, Edith. Nina can do it when she puts her mind to it. Thank her for me will you. I'll be down to join you both presently."

"Where are we?" Edith peered through the wheelhouse window.

"We are nearing Port la Nouvelle. I'll anchor here until I've eaten."

"Are you going to get off the boat and stay here for a break?" Edith asked as she went out on the deck to try to identify where they were.

"I doubt it, but you can ask Nina, she usually decides when we go ashore."

Edith returned to the lounge to find Nina lying back against the couch. On the tray added to the empty breakfast dishes was a wine glass a third full with a dark red liquid.

"Do you want more coffee?"

"Yes, of course I do, I told you I would." She indicated the glass. I had to get a drink for myself."

What was in the girl's glass appeared to be port. Removing it and leaving it on the coffee table, she picked up the tray with its dirty crockery. Moving into the galley, she replenished the kettle. Rinsing out the cup, she made another coffee, pouring the remaining hot water into the sink.

As she took the coffee into Nina, Simon arrived with his tray. Edith took it from him, noting with satisfaction that he too had cleared all she had prepared for him.

"I am going to wash the dirty dishes," she said. As she left them, she heard Nina say, "When are you going to do it?"

Just what was Simon going to do, she wondered.

Chapter 19

Quietly Edith put down the tray and crept back to the area between the lounge and the galley, where she could hear the couple talking.

"We're too close to the shore," Simon replied. "We must wait until we're in quieter waters."

"You should get those papers out for signing. I just had to stop her opening that cupboard."

"I'm inclined to agree with you. Perhaps I'll up anchor and travel further out. I tell you what though, I wish we hadn't had such a large meal last night, followed by that assortment of liquor. I'm quite lethargic this morning."

"I'm feeling the same, but you've landed me with looking after her. Incidentally she's very quiet down there. I'd better see what she's doing."

Edith slipped quickly back to the sink. She was wiping Simon's breakfast dishes by the time he got there.

"In the lounge, Edith," he ordered. "We have something for you to do which is more important."

She turned, holding up a plate. "I'll be with you in a few minutes, this is all I have to do."

With his back to her, he opened the small cupboard on his left, removing the case she had discovered earlier and carrying it into the lounge, where he sat next to Nina with it on his lap. Edith followed him in, stopping short when she saw what he held.

"So you found it! My fan cabinet! Oh thank you, Simon! Where did you find it? Oh you are so clever, I search everywhere in my room at Oak..."

"No need to get excited, you stupid woman," Nina interrupted. "It was yours, but it isn't any longer, it's ours. Well at least it will be when you sign it over to us."

"But I have never given it to you, or to Simon, and I do not intend to do so now. You will please to give it to me, Simon." Edith walked forward to take her property from him.

Opening it he removed some papers and handed the case to Nina. After perusing the first of the papers he offered that too to her. "Hold it until I need it," he said. He smiled as he read. Then he stood up, indicating to Edith to move to one of the other seats. She held out her hand for the cabinet, but Simon laughed and pushed her backwards to the seat.

"Don't be awkward. You will sign this paper or I shall hand you over to Nina's tender mercies and I won't answer for the consequences."

He handed Edith the paper. Reluctantly, recovering her spectacles from her shoulder bag and taking care to hang it again over her shoulder, she read the paper with disbelief.

To whom it may concern. This is to authorise Simon Markham to sell on my behalf the cabinet of fans which until this day have been my sole property, having been previously purchased by myself for personal purposes, and which I now relinquish to his care and keeping.

Signed This Day.

"I refuse to sign such a letter. I do not wish you to sell them for me, Simon. Why would I ask you to do such a thing?"

The girl laughed. "You won't be needing them where you're going."

"If I would wish to sell them I will ask my nephew Treve to..."

"That wimp," Simon sneered, "He couldn't sell a bag of beans."

"Don't argue with the stupid cow, Simon," Nina ordered him. "If she won't do it, show her the other letter, we'll get more from that anyway judging by the way those simpering mugs behaved when she went missing for a few hours."

"What do you know of that?" Edith reacted immediately. Surprised, she turned on Simon. "So you were involved, Simon? I knew it was you who pushed me down into the garden, why? Why would you do such a thing to me? We are friends."

Nina sniggered. "Ha, that's what you think. He was never a friend of yours. He was after that nurse who works where you live."

"Maree?"

"Yes. She's the one with the money isn't she?"

"Be quiet, Nina," Simon ordered. "You are tired, you're talking too much."

"Yes, I am tired," she replied. "So get on with it. If she won't sign that, give her this." She held out the other paper. "That's the ransom note. If that precious nurse has got the legacy you claim to have found a copy of in her father's desk, it will be worth a lot more than the stupid fans in that case. We can copy her signature for the fans when she's not around to do it."

"What is she talking about, Simon?" Edith appealed. "She is not permitted to forge my signature. You are a solicitor, you should tell her."

Simon snatched the paper from Nina, thrusting it angrily toward Edith, who let it fall to the floor.

"You too can stop asking questions," he told her. "Read it! If you haven't signed by the time I return it will be sent to your precious nephew and friends. Keep your eye on her Nina, I won't be long."

Edith made no attempt to pick up the paper as Simon left to go back up the stairs. A few minutes went by in silence, then came the sound of the anchor being drawn up.

"You'd better do as he says or you'll be feeding the fish before long," the girl said. Edith ignored her.

"I bet you're wondering how he got hold of that case?" Nina continued. "He reckons it was easy." She yawned. "Ooh I wish you'd sign that paper now. I could do with a sleep." She yawned again. "Yeah, he said you were always going out in the garden climbing trees, he only had to wait till you was up one of them, nip in and help himself. Serves you right."

"But how did he get into my room?" Edith could not prevent herself asking.

"Oh, he had a key cut from a copy he made when a cleaner left her bunch in the reception one day. You're a careless lot. He's got copies of loads of them, so they all better watch out."

Edith said nothing. There was still much she didn't understand. She heard Simon returning.

"It's raining," he said, glancing at the paper, still on the floor where he'd left it. "She's not co-operated then?" He bent down to pick it up, offering it to Edith, who again ignored it.

"Very well," he said. "Come and hold her, Nina. If she needs help we'll give it to her."

As the girl wearily made her way over he grasped Edith by the shoulders, attempting to lift her from the seat. It took the pair of them to get her on her feet. Squirming and kicking, she burst into tears. When they finally got her on to the couch where Nina had been sitting, her crying had turned to loud, noisy sobbing, followed by hysterical shrieks. "Leave me alone!" she shouted.

"Oh for god's sake," said Nina. "Stop her making that row, Simon, she's doin' my 'ead in."

But Edith hadn't forgotten her stage skills. Simon was finding it difficult to keep her under any sort of control. He growled at her to pack the noise in and she retaliated by kicking him in the shins, shouting 'Help!' at the top of her voice and struggling even more violently. Nina had had enough. She let go of her irritating charge.

"Stop it, you stupid bitch, or I'll throw you over the side myself," she snapped. She began to slap Edith around the head and face, but they were weak slaps and had little effect. Edith continued shrieking.

"That'll do, Nina," said Simon. "We don't want hand marks on her face when she's found."

Ordering Nina to hold Edith while he arranged the papers for signing, he released his own tight grip. His words fell on deaf ears. Nina could not have obeyed had she wanted to; the struggle to subdue Edith had finished her. She collapsed in a heap on the floor.

"Oh, Hell, Nina, don't go to sleep on me now, I need your help," he grumbled. Letting go of Edith completely, he bent over the girl. Lifting her, he eased her on to the settee, trying to shake her awake.

Edith dived for the stairs. She was outside and hanging on tightly to the rail when he reached her.

"Touch me and I'll scream," she threatened him when he caught up with her. There were few other boats close by, but this was a busy area, especially at this time of day, and he knew that one could come along at any moment. He didn't fancy tangling with an inquisitive burly fisherman returning from a night at sea.

He made his way to the wheelhouse, needing to think. Damn Nina! Why did she have to let him down now? Well, he'd give her half an hour. She should be ready to help again then.

He too was tired, bloody tired. He yawned and rubbed his eyes to clear them. The damned rain wasn't helping, as the wheelhouse windows were difficult to see through. The wind was getting up too. He would have to keep his wits about him. Though things weren't too serious; he told himself; after all, they were a long way from shore, their unwilling benefactress wasn't going anywhere unless she tried swimming for it and even good swimmers would balk at tackling thirty kilometres, which was how far out from Agde they'd be at Fort Brescou. He had promised to take her out there, hadn't he?

He glanced out to where the woman was still hanging on to the rail. She was getting soaked. Should he tell her to come in? No, of course not, she'd be even wetter in a while. He'd keep a closer eye on her if she was inside. But, he told himself, it was easy to keep her in view from here, and if she couldn't see him she wouldn't realise he too was weary.

Oh damn! she wasn't waiting to be asked! And she'd got the bloody lifebelt, what was she intending using that for?

"I'm standing under cover," she said. "If you come near me I shall jump over."

"Don't be foolish, woman! In this weather you'd never be seen. You'd certainly not be heard and this far out you wouldn't last two minutes."

"I will take my chance. It would be an improvement to staying on this boat with you and that girl who wishes to beat me."

"You should sign the paper. Then we'll leave you alone."

"But I cannot agree to what you are telling me to do. You do not ask my permission to take away my property, now you would force me to give it to you, you make me have the accident at the hotel when I might have seriously hurt myself, and somebody takes me away from my friends. I do not understand why all these things happen."

Simon was hearing all this from what seemed like a long way away. He felt himself swaying, and grasped even more tightly on to the wheel.

"Oh shut up prattling, woman, you know what you have to do, and you're making me tired. Go away."

"Then maybe you too should have a little sleep, Simon. Do you wish to go into the lounge with Nina?"

"That would suit you wouldn't it?" he sneered, "to see me fall asleep? And who is going to keep us afloat? We might all drown. That wouldn't be very clever now... would it..." His voice drifted away. Edith watched him carefully. When his whole body relaxed, his hands sliding down either side of the wheel, she lightly grasped his arm.

"Let down the anchor Simon, then you can have a rest and we won't drown, because you will still be in control."

"Tha's right, I will still be the s-s-skipper, tha's true and you can't go anywhere if I drop the little anchor like this, c-c-can you?"

"I will go and see if your friend is awake," Edith said carefully. When he didn't reply, she scampered down below to find the girl prone, as they'd left her. Good, she would keep. Checking the contents of her bag, she gave Simon time to get back behind the wheel before hurrying back up. He was again holding on to the wheel, though still swaying precariously. The boat had stopped.

"Why don't you come and sit outside in the air for a minute or two?" she said. "You will soon recover yourself."

"Thassa clever idea. Are you, um, coming with me?"

"Yes Simon, I will come with you. I'll bring the lifebelt with me, then you won't have to worry about falling overboard."

Grabbing a cushion from inside the wheelhouse, she guided him to the seat in the bows, where he collapsed thankfully. She helped him to sit, and when he showed a tendency to lean his head against the rails she eased him so that he lay along the seat. Placing the cushion under his head, she swung his legs up on to the seat.

"Rest for a while Simon," she said. Reaching into her bag, she removed one of her early-morning purchases; a pair of flesh-coloured tights. Unwrapping them quickly, she spoke quietly to the now sleeping man.

"I am going to make sure you do not slip off the boat and into the water, Simon," she murmured. With the dexterity of a seasoned mariner, she used the tights to secure him to the rails by his wrists, using a second pair for his ankles. She then made her way once more down to the lounge.

"Now my sleeping beauty, I must make sure you do not fall and hurt yourself," she whispered. She used more pairs of tights to secure Nina firmly to the rails of the couch. Then she stood over the prostrate girl.

"And it will not matter if you call, even loudly. He will not come to you," she told her.

Gathering up the loose papers, she pushed them into the fan cabinet, then closed it and placed it at the foot of the stairs and went back in to the galley. Putting on a pair of kitchen gloves, she began to tidy away dishes and dispose of the breakfast debris. She carried two part-bottles of port into the lounge, leaving the one left by Nina earlier tucked in between the seat cushions.

Then Edith collected her fan cabinet, adjusted her shoulder bag and made her way up to the wheelhouse, where she left everything whilst she checked that the knots still held the man securely. Familiarising herself with the controls, she pressed the switch for drawing up the anchor and set the engine in motion, aiming for the Island Fort Brescou. A fine rain still fell, and the wind was light. The tide was ebbing.

As she neared her target, she allowed the boat to drift while she took a couple of photographs. Her watch indicated it was well past the time she should have been returning to Agde.

She removed the white cardigan and the scarf from around her neck. A short flagpole was attached to the front of the wheelhouse. She reached as far as she was able and fastened the cardigan to it by the sleeves. If her friends were watching, they would know she was safe.

Edith enjoyed being at the helm. On a corkboard attached to

the inside wall was a list of the cruiser's capabilities. She read that it was well able to cope with coastal or offshore cruising, so she had no hesitation in continuing with her plan to stay at sea until her passengers began to stir. This holiday had not been all she had anticipated, but today she was in control.

Steering clear of the rocks surrounding the fort, she slowed to a crawl. One more long look at the fort with its lighthouse and it was time to head again for Agde. Swinging the craft to starboard, she began a slow cruise. A couple of miles on, she turned it again toward the fort. Enjoying the power the boat gave her, she continued to drive backwards and forwards, each time aiming a little nearer the shoreline.

Some ten kilometres in, she noticed a fast boat heading in her direction. She slowed down and dashed out to the sleeping man. Then she took out her nail scissors and cut the tights from his arms and legs, stowing them in her bag. Finally she grabbed the lifebelt and put it back in the wheelhouse. Paying a swift visit to the lounge, she performed the same operation on the girl's bonds.

Having returned to the helm, Edith was well in control by the time she recognised the faster craft bearing down on her as a marine patrol boat, driven by a man in naval uniform. Accompanying him were two police officers and a policewoman. As they neared, Edith put the *Maxine Louise* into reverse, slowing to a stop as they drew alongside.

"Ahoy there! Are you Edith Arneau?"

"I am sir, what can I do for you?"

"We'd like to come aboard ma'am."

"Then please do so, officer." Throwing a short rope ladder over the rail, one of the policemen clambered aboard, followed by the other male and the female. The extra engine noise disturbed Simon, who sat up, swinging shaky legs to the deck and attempting to stand. He immediately fell backwards, and would have gone over the side if the policeman nearest had not pressed him back on to the seat.

"Wass going on? Who are you?" He tried again to stand. Again he was pushed back and held down.

"We are English police officers sir," said the leading officer. They all produced official identity wallets. "Are you Simon Markham, owner of this motor cruiser?"

"I am, whass that to do with you?"

"We are acting on the instructions of the English Court Of Justice, sir. We are to accompany you in returning to England." He produced handcuffs and secured Simon to the rails, then turned to Edith.

"Is there anyone else aboard?"

Edith nodded. "Yes , below, a female friend." The officer nodded to his female colleague. "Go below and bring up the woman." On their return, Nina was handcuffed in the same manner.

He then instructed his colleague to take over. "I guess Mrs Arneau has had enough of keeping this boat afloat while its owner slept off his liqueur intake," he said.

Edith relinquished the wheel. "Are my friends at the quayside waiting for me?" she asked.

"Yes Mrs Arneau, they saw your signal and decided to alert us to the fact that it appeared you were ready to come in but there was something amiss, as this craft appeared not to be heading in the right direction. It is obvious now that Mr Markham is in no fit state to be in charge." He glared at the pair, then asked Edith, "Did you notice Mr Markham imbibing a quantity of alcoholic beverage?"

"No sir I did not, but the young lady" - she indicated Nina — "told me they had something called the hair of the dog for breakfast before I came aboard this morning."

They had reached the beach around the corner from Agde harbour. There, a couple of other male officers were waiting to escort the prisoners to a marked car.

Simon tried to bluster his way out of trouble. "I resent your implication, constable, I am perfectly in control. This - this woman - must have knocked me out "

"So that's your story, Mr Markham, do you expect us to believe it? Look at the size of this little lady compared with your own — what, six foot three? You will have to do better than that."

He turned to Edith. "Do you wish to prefer charges against this man in this country before he is transferred to England, ma'am?"

"No, officer, but I wish to have some words with him."

The officer stepped aside, motioning her to carry on. She smiled at the pathetic, bedraggled figure before her.

"Thank you for finding my cabinet of fans, Simon," she said. "I am going to ask these kind policemen to take it to England for me. The letters you allowed me to read on the boat will be placed in the cabinet and lodged in the strong bank. I will never lose them again and I will have the official receipt with today's date stamped on it to always stay at the bank. I am sorry all your plans came to such little success, but you and your girlfriend will soon be having another holiday. I hope you will both enjoy it."

Edith reflected that she would have to buy some more tights next time she went shopping, but first she ought to apologise to everyone at Oaklands for her silly behaviour over the past few weeks. She should not forget to mention the absences when she was having those secret meetings with Antoine.

Thank goodness she was now back to her normal, happy self.

THE END